BLOOD AND STEEL: THE COMPLETE

TALES OF KINGI BWANA, VOLUME 4

BLOOD AND STEEL:
THE COMPLETE TALES OF

KINGI BWANA

VOLUME 4

GORDON
MacCREAGH

ALTUS PRESS • 2014

EDITED AND DESIGNED BY

Matthew Moring

PUBLISHING HISTORY

"A Man to Kill" originally appeared in the November 1938 issue of *Adventure* magazine. Copyright 1938 by Popular Publications, Inc. Copyright renewed 1966 and assigned to Adventure Pulp LLC. All Rights Reserved.

"Slaves for Ethiopia" originally appeared in the July 1939 issue of *Adventure* magazine. Copyright 1939 by Popular Publications, Inc. Copyright renewed 1967 and assigned to Adventure Pulp LLC. All Rights Reserved.

"Strong as Gorillas" originally appeared in the April 1940 issue of *Adventure* magazine. Copyright 1940 by Popular Publications, Inc. Copyright renewed 1968 and assigned to Adventure Pulp LLC. All Rights Reserved.

"Blood and Steel" originally appeared in the June 1940 issue of *Adventure* magazine. Copyright 1940 by Popular Publications, Inc. Copyright renewed 1968 and assigned to Adventure Pulp LLC. All Rights Reserved.

THANKS TO

Doug Ellis, Joel Frieman, Everard P. Digges LaTouche and Gerd Pircher.

TABLE OF CONTENTS

A MAN TO KILL

CAPT. HAWKS of His Majesty's East African police
strode very determinedly towards the little camp under
the shade of the flat, umbrella-top acacias. He was hot under
the collar for reasons more than the slanting sun, and he swore
as he stumbled over the stiff bunch grass tussocks.

"Give this blasted foreigner a healthy surprise. Can't let 'em
come trampling all over regulations any way they jolly well
please."

He was still half a mile from the camp. But the man who
was to be surprised separated himself from behind the tan and
brown broken sunlight of a mimosa trunk and grinned most
amiably at the officer. A tall, hard figure and rangy. Sun tanned
and khaki clad, he looked as though he might have been carved
out of a tough length of that same tree trunk and jointed together with steel wires. He said: "Ah! Come on into the camp,
Sergeant, and sit. Been expecting you for three days. You're just
in time. I'm sort of figuring to shoot a man this night, and I'd
like for you to be a witness."

Thin wrinkles that narrowed the man's eyes progressed into
twin deep grooves to restrict the spread of his lips and extended on down to cut the lean grimness of his jaw.

Captain Hawkes was too suddenly taken back even to unbut-
ton the flap of his pistol holster that regulations prescribed to
be carried—a little ineffectually for a quick draw—snug on the
right side of the tight belt. But he was just as grim as the other,

and very precise. Captain, late of the 72nd Punjabis; sergeant now of the police; but the military precision stuck; not only in the stiff carriage and trim mustache, but in the neat uniform, cut by an English tailor, precisely buttoned and belted—and very hot.

Ex-Capt. Hawkes of the Punjabis was very new in the East African police, and very impatient with the easy going methods of some of the old-timers. But all his military experience had left him incapable of contemplating the possibility of ever having actually to use his gun. The majesty of the law was with him in a land where the Law was something that white men knew to have teeth in it.

The tall man's grin, however, was remaining amiable.

"C'm on in," he said, "and let me give you a drink. It's pretty hot walking until the sun drops below the scrub line."

Determined Sergeant Hawkes was, but not unnecessarily hostile.

"Well, I'll do that," he said. "I'll take your drink; but I'm warning you, you'll do no shooting for a while. I'm arresting you for shooting that elephant."

"Oh! About that elephant?" The man's hard grin remained as though it had been carved in to stay.

An enormous black man heaved himself up from his hunkers in front of the tent and threw off the blanket that Africans *will* wear whenever doing nothing.

Splendidly naked, the man wore only a leopard-skin apron and fringed garters of monkey hair flowing from little spurs at elbow and knee. He saluted with a spear that had a blade nearly three feet long.

"By Jove!" Sergeant Hawkes' hard eyes bored keenly at the formidable shape. "What kind of a native is that?" Hawkes' speech was no indication of sissiness; it was just his heritage of a military aristocracy.

"Masai. An *Elmorani wa-simba-muuwaji.*"

"An *elmor*—what?"

*"Speak to him,
Barounggo."*

"Meaning he's killed his lion single-handed with a spear."

"Hmfh! And—good Lord! What's this one?" The sergeant's eyes were adjusting themselves to the sudden dimness of the tent after the blinding sun. "This fellow a trained monkey or something? Not a pigmy, is he? They tell me you can't make servants of those chaps. Sort of a freak show you have here, Mr.—er—what?"

"Hottentot. And as smart as the other is savage. And the name, Sergeant, is King."

THERE WERE officers in Africa who would have stopped to do a lot of thinking. But that name meant nothing to Sergeant Hawkes. He swilled his drink around in the glass and looked through its murky flatness as though it were the rarest of wine—it was lemon, squeezed into the lukewarm melange of liquids that comes from a water hole where animals drink.

"Aa-ah!" The sergeant gulped the half of it.

"People call me Kingi Bwana."

The sergeant gulped the remaining half. "Aa-ah! That was a life-saver. And I'll have another of the same, if you don't mind. Almost sorry to have to take you in. Mr. King."

King said only: "I'm beginning to suspect, Sarge, you're sort o' new in the country."

The Hottentot was smart enough to know all the symptoms. Another drink was waiting.

"New here," Hawkes admitted cheerfully. "But experienced enough to know how to tap you on the shoulder and warn you that anything you say may be used against you."

King was just as cheerful. "We'll come to that later. For the present there's more important things, like this man that I think I'll have to shoot."

Hawkes could see the humor of that. "Ha-ha! You bally Yankees, I understand, have an idea that you can spoof your way out of getting what you call a ticket, eh? Not with us, Mr. King. You can't go shooting an elephant in a British colony without a license and not have us jump you. I'd have been here even sooner if the dashed plane hadn't set me down at the wrong camp."

"When you're older in the country," King grinned, "you won't try to spoof me with that kind of yarn. Bush telegraph reported three days ago that you were coming to look into the disappearance of Ogilvie."

"Bush telegraph? Dash it all, my dear sir, you don't swallow that, do you? Though some of the old-timers at H.Q.—What do you know about Ogilvie?"

"Ogilvie was a very good friend of mine. Pulled me out of a fuss with a lion once, and got himself clawed close to the limit. A whole white man, Ogilvie. I just heard about him. Been away myself for a couple of years—up in this mess that's Italian Ethiopia these days."

"Ethiopia? Then that means you've come without a passport too. Damn it, Mr. King, some of you foreign blighters just don't seem to realize that international boundaries are serious things nowadays, and the Law is— This is a lot more serious than just an unlicensed elephant."

"A whole lot more serious. Like this man I'm telling you about that I want you to be witness when I—"

"Don't play the fool, Mr. King." Sergeant Hawkes' patience was used up. "I'm sorry, but I've got to arrest you."

KING STILL grinned and lounged his length on a chop box over his cot. The sergeant sat on a similar chop box at the tent flap.

"Well, all right then," King said. "Let's be serious. What are you going to arrest me with?"

"What I'm going to—" The significance of the insinuation required some time to take hold. He stared at King. Then, "Oh, well, if you put it that way—" Not very expertly he unbuttoned the flap of his holster and produced the service revolver. "I'm sorry you make me do it this way."

The grin remained confident on King's face.

"Now I'd say," he told the sergeant judicially, "you're a pretty good type of athletic Britisher. You've played a lot of polo in your military service, and you've shot tigers in India. All in all, you're probably a good man with a rifle. But your regulations never teach you fellows anything about small gun play. You're slow as glaciers."

Sergeant Hawkes said: "You can't fool me, my good man, by looking over my head, behind me. I know about that trick."

King said: "Speak to him, Barounggo."

"*Haya!*" A great voice boomed over the sergeant's head and cool metal touched his neck. The flat of it slid along his skin until a foot of spear blade stood out under his chin, where he could see it without dropping his eyes from King's.

"And even if I didn't have him—" King said. "Look, I'll show you something about guns." He made a blurred movement to his shirt front, under his arm, and the sergeant was looking at a flat little blue automatic. "I'll bet you wouldn't even have frisked me for this. You fellows rely a heap too much on the majesty of your law—and you're a long way away from it just now." He laughed and threw the automatic onto the camp table. "Come on, Sergeant, I'm not fighting the British Colonial Empire. I got more important things to do this night. Put up your gun and call it even—until tomorrow, and we can argue about elephants again." His gun was shameless.

Sergeant Hawkes was brave enough, but not a fool. He put his regulation revolver on the table.

"You're being a bloody idiot," he said. "And I'm not giving in. I warn you, I'm going to arrest you."

"As inflexible as glaciers," King grinned. "Yeah, your crowd has the reputation of getting your man, same's your Canadian bunch. So I'll warn you, tomorrow you'll be sending for reinforcements."

"If it takes the British army," Hawkes said curtly. "We'll take you, my dear fellow. Don't you worry."

"Oh, I'm not. By the way, who was it informed you about that elephant business?"

"A native, name of Mosha. I happened to be at Todali outpost, and I had the Port Sudan plane detour me off here."

King nodded, looking narrow-eyed into the hazy nothings of dusk. "Ah, Mosha, was it? So nobody has killed Mosha yet? A good runner, that fellow; a four-day trek for him to Todali. Went to a lot of trouble to inform, didn't he? If old Sarge Rowland had been at Todali, he'd have been wondering about that. I'll be attending to Mosha." He shrugged his wide shoulders out of a dark reminiscence. "But come, come. Darkness deepens, and we have a man to shoot. Your duty as a police officer compels you to come along and stop me. You agree, it's a truce till tomorrow?" His cheerfulness was false. There was a deadly seriousness underneath it.

The sergeant said: "I think the sun's hit you in the head. But I'm coming, of course. And all right—it's half time till tomorrow."

"O.K. Your word on that goes with me. Better maneuver that gun of yours into its case. You'll be needing a rifle. I'll loan you one. You look hard enough to do a fast ten miles yet tonight, even on top of the six or so from that trader camp where the plane dropped you."

"Do twenty, my dear chap, to keep you in sight," Sergeant Hawkes growled.

King gave quick orders. To the Hottentot: "Kaffa, the usual precautions. Only that you will shoot any visitors more than the *askaris* can handle."

The usual precautions meant that Kaffa would perch, apelike, in a tree, from where the surprise value of sudden bullets upon dumb raiding spearmen would be immense.

"Barounggo, the soldier rifle for the Polis *Bwana*. Plant out your night guard, and we go."

THE MASAI handed Hawkes a heavy-stocked military rifle and a cartridge pouch and went out to bully his men. King grinned again at the policeman's indignation. "Yes, yes, I know. Your regulation .308, and it's against your regulations that I should have it; but that's the one you'll use best, if you have to—which, Mister, I'm hoping for both of us you won't."

The great Masai was ominously growling at the *askaris*. Eight of them; fine stalwarts. He had picked them and trained them under his own ruthless driving, but he remained ever dissatisfied of their performance. Porters they had been originally, gawky oxen with nothing other than strength to recommend them; and they still carried the loads necessary for King's meager camps and covered distances with them that the ponderous *safaris* of less hardened travelers would never believe. But the contemptuous designation of *wa-pagazi* they had shed, for the Masai had beaten into their beings the miracle of putting spears into their hands and making fighting men of them, *askaris*.

Obediently they were disposing of themselves around the camp fringe as sentries.

Hawkes hazarded the remark, half incredulous: "How long will they stay there after we're out of sight, if a lion comes roaring round? Or the ghosts that these African chappies seem to fear more than anything else?"

"Pity you haven't got the Swahili as yet." King told him. "His last exhortation, I mean. He was telling 'em: 'If trouble comes and the camp suffers, let no man of you be alive when I return'."

"Hmfh! Another ruffian who thinks he's far from the Law. And you're expecting to get trouble?"

"Nope. Excepting to make it. Just being cautious here."

King set a stiff pace into the low hills that were already black against the last purple of the sky. "Got to make time in the open. We'll not have to bother about lion trouble here."

"No? Well, I'm glad you're so certain about lions at night, too."

King chuckled out of the dimness ahead. "I figured they'd be in the back of your mind, and yet you got the guts to tag along anyhow. You'll learn to be a cop yet, soldier. About lions: there's been no game in sight for three days, so they'll be wherever the meat's gone. So we can hike right along here; we'll hit rain forest and wash ravines in those hills, and then we can afford to slow up. The killing isn't due till high of moon."

Sergeant Hawkes was toughly skeptical. "You don't spoof me with that killink talk, my dear man, even if I don't know yet what this madness is."

King's voice came back without the chuckle. "This is Africa.

And there's things that a white man's *got* to do in Africa. Come ahead, tough guy."

S E R G E A N T   H A W K E S   had no immediate comment. This King fellow talked with a coldblooded callousness that made the possibility of anything serious seem far and improbable. And yet the hardness of that grim face didn't look as though it invented ghost stories. If it laughed, it laughed at the precariousness of life just as it did at the seriousness of official regulations. Damned exasperating, but—

"Blasted efficient sort of a beggar." His conclusion grunted from him as he stumbled along.

"Huh?" said King's tall shadow from ahead.

Hawkes was still thinking. A vague recollection was coming to him of something he had heard.

"Would you be that King fellow who used to be in this country and of whom they said, wherever he was there was trouble?"

"No sirree!" King's voice sounded genuinely alarmed. "Don't let anybody give me that kind of a rep. I'm the Kingi Bwana that was born into the ill luck to be often enough where trouble was. Ask your chief at Nairobi; he'll tell you."

"And then the trouble usually cleared up? By Jove, I'm remembering about some of those stories."

"This one won't." King's voice was suddenly grim and hard. "Not till you dig in and clear it up yourself. I'm telling you, Mister, you've dropped out of the sky into a party."

The moon was showing over the scrub tops now, white and big enough to be blamed for the heat of the night. It helped Sergeant Hawkes a lot. King and the Masai stalked along as though they walked by the feel of the ground underfoot, like elephants, and as silently. Hawkes was sweating a pint per mile. He was glad when King called a breathing halt at the base of a dark rounded boulder that stood incongruously alone, in the middle of the empty rolling grass land.

King mopped his face. The Masai seemed to be as incapable of perspiration as an iron statue.

"If they'd had the decency," King said, "to wait a month, you'd be using a blanket."

"Who are 'they'? What's all this bally lunatic mystery?"

"It's an interesting thing," King said. "Talking about glaciers and you British. How this rock ever got here. This is the edge of the great African rift. Something in the old red hot days went boom and split the continent pretty near in half. There never was a glacier to roll rocks along and leave 'em lying along its front. Yet you'll find things like this every now and then for miles."

"Really, my dear chap, I can't get interested just now," Hawkes grumbled. "What's African geology got to do with a white man crazy in the African night and me following him like a bally ass?" And he added the logical thought: "Why don't I just pot you from behind for a homicidal maniac?"

"Regulations, copper," King derided him. "Your hide-bound Law don't let you. Now in my own country a tough cop would call this a kidnaping and take me in on a stretcher."

"Savages," Hawkes grunted.

"Yeah." King said dryly. "We're going to meet some, and you'll see what savages are like. You'll learn, Britisher, how good is your Law and your regulations at the far ends of 'em. Come ahead. We got to watch that moon for straight shooting."

CHAPTER II

DRUMS OF DEATH

THE RAIN forest began like a sudden wall. There was no gradual merging of trees into the grass land. A wall of timber stood like an irregular palisade, white in the moonlight, leaving the black shadows of a Dantesque inferno between. But

*The axe head
swished again.*

no tangling vines yet. A breeze, gratefully cool, drifted out of
the woods.

The Masai lifted his head and sniffed the high air with broad
twitching nostrils. You could almost see his ears set forward,
animal-wise, to catch vagrant currents of sound. He grunted.

"*I-me-maliki.*"

"Means, 'They have commenced the business'," King translated.

"Commenced what?"

"I can't hear it myself yet, but it'll be ju-ju drums."

"Meaning what?"

King's head was turned to catch the sound. Hawkes could

not see his face in the shadow, but his voice was as cold and as harsh as a file. "Meaning that a man is going to die this night, pretty horribly. Unless we can stop it—which we can't."

Hawkes' skin suddenly tingled.

"How d'you know anybody is going to die? What I mean, the way you say?"

"I don't absolutely know. Nobody knows for sure about ju-ju, except the devils that's in it. And only the toughest cops butt into it. But me—By God, I *got* to butt in."

King jerked his shoulder to throw his rifle sling from it; automatically, his face drawn in tight lines of thought, he opened his rifle and thumbed the breech to assure himself of a full load. He shrugged his preoccupation from him and tried to talk with the old carelessness. But it was not very convincing.

"Tough enough to tag along, copper?"

"I'm keeping you in sight, Chappie. Don't forget I've arrested you."

"Stiff-necked egg, ain't you. Okay, never mind African geology for just now; you'll get interested in that later. Right now African anthropology is your business. This marks tribal borders. Plains men, like plains animals, won't come in here; because the tree devils, you'll understand, jump on the back of their necks out of the dark."

Hawkes was unconsciously whispering. "By holy Jove! I'll believe 'em. Anything could happen in these shadows."

"Just about anything will." There was mirth in his voice. "These people are Wallegas, two and a half times as primitive as your nomad cattle farmers, and that's saying plenty of words."

With the trees the terrain changed as though heaved out of the plain by the thrust of giant roots. As suddenly as the tree fringe, there was a ridge of shale rock, and beyond it rising ground, and, cut by the rain into the rising ground, little gullies. Later, deep and darkly impenetrable ravines.

The Masai, flitting in advance from shadow to shadow, like some great ogre, peered into the yawning crevasses, lay on his belly to sniff into them for local whiffs of the things that die in African gullies. Uncannily, using all the animal senses that supplement vision in the dark, he remembered locations that he had traversed before, whether it would be practical to climb down the steep sides and up again without breaking a limb or whether one would have to skirt the edges to find a better place. Sometimes the better place would not be for a mile.

Fitful gusts of air carried the growl of the drums, throbbing to crescendo waves, and carried them away again till you could not know whether you still heard drums or whether the insects of the night jungle had been hypnotized by the impelling repetition to buzz and thrum in the same diabolical vibration. But enough of the persistent cadences came over.

"Yeah," King breathed. "That beat means a killing for this night at top moon. C'm on."

THE MASAI felt and snuffled his way through a dark terrain growing ever steeper and craggier, until the throb of the drums prevaded the air all about them, thrown back and sublimated by rocky echoes so that there was no longer any conception of direction.

The vibration was a live thing in the air, a thing to be felt on the skin as well as heard. The repetition of its rhythm fairly beat into a man's senses. It was all new to Hawkes, and a little frightening. He whispered his feeling.

"I've heard Hindu drumming in India, and that can be sort of intoxicating. But this—I can jolly well imagine how this would whip up a man to any bloody madness."

"Yeah," King said. "There's all the devils of old Africa in this. And African devils live on blood, red and hot."

The Masai climbed a steep rise to peer over, a grotesque, gorilloid shadow, spread-eagled in a moonlit patch. He turned and beckoned the white men on.

They scrambled up, and as their heads topped the rise the thunder of drums hit them like gunfire. Hawkes' impulse was to duck.

*Pistol empty,
he smashed his
rifle butt.*

King laughed harshly. "It may yet be just as dangerous." And to the Masai: "Good work, Barounggo. There will be a stick of tobacco upon our return, if—"

A black ravine fell away before them—they could not tell how deep. But intermittently, between waves of drumming, they could hear running water, quite far down.

Across the ravine, at a height almost directly across from them, on what seemed to be a wide shelf, a great fire blazed. From the recesses of solid shadow around it the drums roared out.

But King was not looking at that just now. He was peering into the ravine, listening to the water. Dubiously he muttered:

"It may be a life-saver yet. Deep and steep, and hell dark. Ought to give us a good ten minutes start, maybe fifteen." And, stubbornly: "Damn, a good man ought to be able to run away from all Africa with fifteen minutes start." He drove his elbow at Hawkes. "Look there, copper. There's something that your Law never sees—And the moon, like I said, is just about overhead."

Hawkes, of course, had looked over there first of all; but, not knowing what to look for, he had understood nothing of the devil doings. His attention had wandered back to King's mutterings. He could sense tension in the air, but not the closeness of death. He did not know that, all unconsciously, he was trying to emulate King's coldly callous approach to impending violence.

"Macabre sort of setting, isn't it, old man? What's it all about, and what mad thing are you proposing to do?"

"Propose to shoot into a full moon ju-ju and then see how fast we can all of us run." King shoved his hard-set chin out across the ravine. "Look over there. Hell, what else can we do?"

ACROSS THE pit of the ravine, as it might be in a far amphitheater, the great fire burned a yellow circle out of the crowding shadows. Posturing shapes flitted intermittently before it in black silhouette. An endless line of them, leaping high, bending low to crawl belly flat, in all the African conceptions of deviltry.

Far enough to be flattened and silenced by distance, it looked like something unreal, like a filmed representation of hell. Only that the wind brought the ceaseless waves of the drums, thundering and ebbing; and with their ebb came hoarse, horrid screams.

"There? D'you see it?" King gripped Hawkes' arm; his voice was as thin and tense as a plucked wire.

"By Jove! What kind of business is it?"

"You don't see it. Watch over the fire as the drums let down. That's so they can enjoy the shrieking."

The drum waves ebbed again, and Hawkes saw now a frame

that looked like a cross; a thing that staggered drunkenly on insecure footing and threw an unholy lurching shadow on the ruddy back-drop of fire-lit trees. Its fitful movements seemed to be controlled by men who raised and lowered it with ropes.

It lowered with a hellish deliberation over the fire again, and in the bright glow Hawkes could see now a darker blot attached to it that screeched horribly.

"By God! It's—" Hawkes' voice caught in his throat. Studied casualness was gone. "Is it a man?"

"That one," said King, "will be Ogilvie's head boy!"

"Good God! How d'you know? Why—what hellish thing is happening?"

King's voice seemed to Hawkes incredibly cold and deliberate.

"Head boy was a mission convert. The cross is just African humor."

Hawkes had no such cold-blooded hesitation. He swung his body over the lip of the ravine. "We can get there in time to stop it."

King grabbed his sleeve and dragged him back.

"You can't. Nobody can. There's a thousand black men there, drunk with drums and the *madawa* drug, all howling blood-mad."

"But good Lord—"

"There's no good Lord in African ju-ju. I've seen one of you nervy Britishers walk into a native village single-handed and drag your man out by the ear—in daylight. But there's nobody can fool with a ju-ju crowd on their own mad night."

"Then—what can we do?"

"So I figured," King said, very coldly and very methodically, "I'd have to shoot him at long range. I wanted you along as a witness. And if we can get clear with our own skins afterwards, that'll be our good luck.

Hawkes stared at him.

"Or maybe you had better," King said. "You're an officer."

Hawkes' eyes were big. They stayed fixed, as though glassy with death themselves.

King's cold deliberation broke. He flared out at the policeman: "Man, d'you have to debate the question while they torture him?"

Hawkes voice croaked at last from his throat.

"I couldn't do it."

"Damn your regulations!" King snarled at him. "The hell with anything that's so hidebound that—"

Hawkes flared back at him: "Ah, shut your dashed Yankee yelping. I'd do it in a minute. Only I couldn't. Of course it's justified. But—darkness, distance, an' all. We can't sit here taking pot shots at the poor devil. How much time would that mob give us?"

King glowered at him. The Masai spat out into the darkness: "These be an ape people, for only the rock baboons delight in doing hurt. Slaying indeed is a little thing. I in my time have—"

"Peace, slaughterer!" King told him; and with that he got a grip again on his nerves. "Okay, Britisher. If you got the guts to make your own where your Law don't reach— What'd you make the range?"

Again Hawkes was staring at him. "You mean you'll—Good Lord, it'll be incredible shooting! All of six hundred."

King shook his head. "Four-fifty—hope to God."

He lifted his rifle to his ear and listened while he clicked the Lyman sight to that elevation. "And you're a witness. There's a smart voodoo chief over there would send a hundred blacks to swear to murder; and I've seen your impartial British justice hang a white man on less evidence."

He shuffled to find a place where he could lie prone on his belly. The thunder of the drums ebbed and awful shrieks floated across the black ravine.

Hawkes' breath shivered in his throat. "Hurry up, man."

BUT KING was chillingly slow in making sure. He took a little vial from his pocket and dabbed a spot of luminous paint on his front sight. "Going to be damned little time for miss and try again. Barounggo, old night watcher, how far say you?"

The Masai's opinion had no hesitation. "A distance that I can run while the gray crane cries twelve times."

"And that's as good as a clock." King muttered into his rifle butt. "He makes it four hundred. But he always thinks he can run faster'n anybody else. I'll stick to four-fifty."

He composed himself rigid to wait through the drumming thunder until it would ebb and the grisly cross would descend once more over the fire's light. Hawkes' eyes strained out towards the far leaping devil forms and he held his breath as tense as though it was he who aimed. Taut and ready to snap. Minutes!

He had aimed a rifle at men before now—at black men and brown men and white men. But that had been different; that had been duty, patriotism, orders from his country to kill. The responsibility came down from the highest, spread over many shoulders. That was Law. Here he felt that the responsibility lay on his shoulders alone. He, an officer, was giving the order.

Hours! He held his breath. He could hold it not one more throb of his pulse that pounded in his ears. The cross dipped over the blaze that crouched, waiting for it, and now sent long red devil tongues out to lick at it. The agonized shriek came over the ravine. And King fired.

The shriek cut mercifully off. The drums muttered on; their beaters had heard nothing.

The cross dipped into the licking lips of the flame and staggered upwards again, as though its own tendons were seared to distortion. And then, at the lack of its shrieking response, a confused yelling began.

It swelled in volume to howl down the crescendo of the drums; to spread until it seemed that the whole further hillside was howling surprise and rage out of its infernal shadows.

"Golly, what luck!" King heaved himself to his feet. "Jump

now, copper, while the going's dark and bad. Hear 'em! There must be two-three thousand. And thank Pete for this good black ravine. Damned if I don't think we'll get clear."

It was a mad and bruising race down the black hillside. Into gullies, along their rocky bottoms, out where the going seemed better. The first fifteen minutes of it with not a sound of pursuit.

"Could it be," Hawkes panted, "that the sudden miracle of that shot has scared the swine?"

"Wait," King said. "I mean, come on."

In a little while there was no possibility of hopeful guessing. A wave of brute howling came down the wind as the first hunters climbed the lip of the ravine that had blanketed all sound. More howling all along a wide line as others topped the rise.

"That's a good fifteen minutes start." King grunted. "More'n I hoped. And as long as we don't make too much racket they won't know any better'n general direction in the dark—and they'll scatter to cover a wide front."

The Masai cursed the complicated oaths of his kind. "May hyenas dig up my forebears. *Bwana.* This is disgrace to melt a spear. Never have I fled from apes before. May sewage run in my veins. Here, *Bwana,* is a good place to stop and give battle."

"All the Elmorani are mad," King told him. "As they must be ever to make their manhood test against a lion. Stay thou and fight. As for me, I run." To Hawkes he panted: "It's plenty I've run in my time, and plenty it'll be again. How about you, Britisher? What about this ballyhoo that a British soldier never runs?"

In King's ability to mock again at sacred things was a comforting indication, now, of escape. But Hawkes could see no humor in it. He grunted, between gasps: "It's been in history, Yank, that they've run. But never, by God, that they haven't come back."

"Chances look now like you'll live to fight another day, if we once make the plains country."

AND REACH the open plains they did, though the howls of the wide-spread pack followed them right to the black edge of the tree belt. Plentifully bruised they were, with their faces and bare knees slashed by springy branches to copious bleeding. But alive.

King was able to grin once more between huge breaths. "Phe-e-ew! Ain't run that much since me and some Ethiops chased the Eyetalian army at Shebbeli. We can let up a bit now. Those monkeys won't know but what some good herdsmen might be laying for 'em in this territory. Thank Pete, I've said more'n once, for hereditary enmities—which your holy government knows about, too, and plays both ways across the board."

Hawkes remained sturdily dense to levity.

"My government knows enough," he growled, "to jump very fast on that sort of deviltry."

"That's talkin', copper. And, come camp, I hope your conscience'll let you sleep as well as I will. I'm telling you, fella, we've had us a day."

For all of which, long after Hawkes had flung himself onto King's camp cot and dozed into nightmares, they kept waking him up to hear King prowling outside amongst his *askari* sentries.

"So it's not so dashed safe as you like to make out," he murmured out of his hazy exhaustion when King's dark silhouette stooped under the tent flap.

"Just being cautious," King told him. "Just a mite careful."

In the morning Hawkes was profuse with his apologies. "Dash it all, old man, I slept in your cot all night, while you—I don't know—'pon my word, I was so tuckered that I didn't know what—"

King was astoundingly cheerful this bright morning. "In my country," he grinned at Hawkes, "a cop never explains to a prisoner. Today is tomorrow, and you're arresting me for crimes—elephants and unlawful entries and what not."

Hawkes remained stolid. "You said it yourself, Yank. That

will come later, rest assured. There are more important things just now. I've jolly well got to go back and teach that voodoo chief a thing or two."

King chuckled. "But there was something else I said: Today you'll be sending for reinforcements."

Hawkes scowled at him and drummed his fingernails against his front teeth. "You mean, I couldn't—we couldn't snaffle this blighter together?"

"Ho? It's we, is it? You figurin', copper, I aim to shove my face into that mess again?"

For the first time Hawkes grinned at him. "You know dashed well, you ungodly bounder, I couldn't shove you out of it."

King's grin was as hard and as bleak as ever, because the contours of his face were that way; but there was just a shade of difference to it. He was genuinely pleased.

"Well, now!" he said.

"But I'm not condoning the other things." Hawkes could remain impartially friendly about that. "I've got to uphold the Law, old man."

Impiousness came back to King's grin. "Inflexible is the word, ain't it. Well, set and let's coffee up and I'll tell you about it. And first lemme tell you for a treat that this Hottentot makes *coffee*. Times are, I almost figure the mission laid on me by the Lord is to travel around Africa and let my Hottentot teach you Britishers how to brew a real drink."

H E S A T on his chop box and breathed in the aroma of a brew that even Hawkes admitted was not so bad. King lit his pipe and fired a didactic finger at Hawkes like a gun.

"Now listen. I've seen British guts pull off some hair-raisin' things in Africa. But you're up against a tough layout here. These Wallegas are pretty far on the edge of things, and they don't know so much about the old British Lion."

"It's time they were taught."

"Time and past. But look. That village is ju-ju headquarters.

There'll be, judging from the spread of last night's yelping, a couple of thousand tribesmen gathered from around the hills; and that's a little more'n just prestige can handle. These Wallegas are some different from your tame Kavirondos and Wakambas and all these plains fellows."

"Well then," Hawkes said doggedly, "if it takes the British army."

"Good old Pax Britannica. But the old British army, as you won't admit, but everybody else knows, takes as long a time to get moving as a steam roller."

"But it keeps moving ahead." Hawkes defended instantly.

"Granted, most of the time. But you can't go ponderously official here. There's complications."

"What complications? The thing, in the long run, is a simple case of law enforcement. These swine have committed a brutal crime; they must be taught their lesson."

"And damn well will be." King's agreement was suddenly grimly vengeful. "But listen. Ju-ju runs in threes. Too deep for me to know just why; but there's a scientific sharp I know is writing a whole book, 'The Persistence of the Trinity Theory in African Theomorphy', which is a whole mouthful of words. But it means that three nights from now, or mid-moon of the last quarter, another jamboree is due."

Hawkes sat looking at King with widening eyes, nervously turning the tip of his trim mustache.

"And Ogilvie had two other servants! Loyal British subjects!"

"Good God!" Hawkes remained frozen; only his finger tips twisted with a tiny grating sound on his mustache tip.

King leaned over the little camp table, firing a fierce question that crackled like fast shooting.

"You got the guts, copper, to swing your own bat, hard and fast? Take a responsibility on your own?"

Hawkes stared at the pointing finger, as though held up by it to deliver all he had. He began to nod. Slowly at first, then doggedly.

"Yes, I— Dammit, by George, of course. That's what white officers are for, to take responsibility when higher orders are not available."

"Good lad. What's the best you can do in three days?"

It was an ultimatum as suddenly shocking as a death sentence.

Hawkes considered it, drumming his nails on his teeth. "I've got two native constables at the Todali outpost."

King cursed the meagerness of the colonial system. "Two men to look after a district as big as Texas! But—" He began to nod, too, in dour disgust. "Your two and my eight *askaris* makes ten. The Masai is as good as five. The Hottentot can shoot pretty well, and a couple of the *askaris* know how to bang off a gun."

It all sounded utterly mad. A handful against a tribe. But black men led by white prestige had accomplished miracles in Africa before.

"Look. Flag down that return plane and write a noteful of all the authority you got. Order him to heave out mail and bring back your two cops; and tell him to heave out more mail and bring spare guns and all the old uniforms in the locker. If they don't fit the size of my men, it don't matter. We'll rip 'em up the back and tie 'em on. Uniforms carry an awful punch of authority."

Hawkes was being carried into the sweep of the dynamic current. "By Jove, that'll be quite an army, what?"

King grinned back at him. "Look, now. The plane detoured you. Its track'll be passing about fifty miles east. You sit and pack your letter with dynamite. I'll get the Masai ready to carry it—call his brag about how good he can run. He'll do it all right; and he has sense enough to tear up sheets and peg out an S.O.S. on the grass where the pilot can't miss it."

CHAPTER III

"OUR BACKS THEY WILL NEVER SEE!"

THREE DAYS was long waiting, when the momentous and only subject of discussion was the madness of raiding a tribe with fourteen men all told. Hawkes, with military precision, wanted to plan a campaign. King scouted the thought.

"What can you plan? There are no rifle pits and trenches and barbed wire to crash through. Bamboo huts and garbage piles, that's an African village. There's no staff headquarters to capture and paralyze the brains of the enemy. All you can plan is surprise—and the jolt of that is worth half their force, because they'll never suspect we'd have the nerve."

"But my dear chap, you've got to tell your men what to do."

King wouldn't listen. "Tell your two. Mine know what to do—jump in and shoot or spear everything they can see as long as they can stand. That's the way the African fights. It takes ten years of drill to make a machine soldier of him."

"But—"

"And I'll tell you this more about Africans that's all to our good. A daylight African is a lot tamer than a mid-moon African crazy with ju-ju drums and witch doctory."

"Well, that's something to be jolly well thankful for. Still—"

"And here's something more that counts their numbers down. Between jamborees a lot of 'em will be back in their own villages, getting grub; for the African has never been able to organize a commissariat. And the men left in this village will be getting over their ju-ju drug; it'll take long minutes to soak into their thick heads just what's happening. Surprise. That's the only thing we can plan. Surprise 'em at hot noon and sock 'em."

Hawkes laughed with an excitement that was mounting, perforce, to the reckless. "Dashed if I don't think we can make a go of it, old man."

"Hell!" said King. "They'll be a bare five hundred of 'em."

Hawkes' precise training still had worries. "D' you think your Masai boy made the fifty run in time? D' you think the plane spotted his S.O.S.? D' you think—"

"What you got to worry about is whether the pilot accepted your order."

"Oh, he'll do that. My word, I made it strong."

A N D T H E pilot did. With dusk of the third day two native constables tramped in, loaded down with guns and clothing like a pair of junk men and complaining in thick-lipped half English about their dignity as soldiers being ruined by the disgrace of porterage.

They brought a note from the pilot. Typically British. "Sorry I couldn't drop your johnnies any nearer, old man. No possible landing terrain. Wish I could come with you on your binge. Luck."

Hawkes could still find incompleted details. "What about the Masai getting back? Fifty and back is a lot of foot slog."

"He'll be back. It's not so much for a good runner." King grinned with tight lips. "By the same token friend elephant-informer Mosha will be home in time for the killing that's been due him these couple of years."

The Masai came in sure enough, some time during the night, and, iron man that he was, he was up and haranguing his *askaris* with the dawn. It was a long speech, full of grandiloquent brag about his own past exploits that must be a shining example to them, and of blood chilling threats of his wrath, should they not make it so. The gist of it all, the not-to-be-forgotten ultimum, was:

"You, whom I picked from the jungles as cattle and made into *askaris,* you have beside you two soldiers of the *Bertisi Serkali.* Let no man of you show a lesser killing than they."

The *askaris* yelled and leapt in the air, slapping their buttocks and shadow-fighting their spears.

King chuckled at Hawkes over the enameled coffee cups. "You fellows will never do it, of course, but that's the stuff that hits the African in the fighting spot."

Hawkes, of course, was on the immediate defensive. "We manage to do pretty well with our fellows, I think."

"In ten years." King laughed at him. "Yeah, with ten years of drill you can beat a little white man discipline into the African skull. Barounggo has had these lads in hand barely one—and you watch 'em fight, soldier."

Hawkes laughed too. "Hope so, old fellow. We'll need it."

Even the *askaris* were able to laugh. Gripped by that mysterious exhilaration that comes to fighting men about to meet odds, they guffawed at their own grotesque fitting into old uniforms too small for their bulk, ripped and laced with strings. And they made the old boast of soldiers, whatever their color, the world over.

"Let but the fronts be whole, Bwana. Our backs they will never see."

And one ebullient egoist started a scramble for the better garments, announcing confidently: "For each man that I slay I take me one such golden medal of the *Beritisi Serkali* to make me a necklace." He meant the lion and unicorn-monogrammed uniform buttons.

"By Jove," Hawkes admired, "they've got the right spirit."

"Yeah." King looked them over critically. "Uniforms. That's one thing you British have done. You've taught Africa that your uniform can't be licked. Let's get going. Take it easy before the day's heat hits the plains, and save our breath for the big rush."

IN THE daylight jungle, Hawkes was continually aghast at the rocky steepness of the gullies they had so precipitately traversed by night.

"With the devil on his tail," King grinned, "a man can do

things." But the grin was tightening up on his face. It was a contortion of his lips and eye corners; there was nothing of humor to it.

By daylight one gully could be found leading into another. The raiding party, grimly silent all of them, followed the bottoms. Never on a sky line, never on any ridge where the wind could catch and carry a sound or scent. Running water told them when they were in the big ravine.

"Surprise," King muttered. "And the luck is running with us. Better find the first ford, Barounggo, and keep on their side."

They crept along as silently as animals in bare feet. King, in moccasin-soled Adirondac boots, Hawkes, in regulation hard leather footwear, made an appalling racket over loose stones and rubble; but the wind, of course, filtered down the ravine.

They came to a place where refuse littered the ravine side in an accumulated avalanche of the years, the inevitable signature of an African community. Above them, straggling like a monkey roost along a rock ledge where they could not see it, must be the ju-ju village.

King looked to Hawkes and nodded, pointing up with his eyebrows. All unnecessarily, of course; he did not even know that his own tension was out-functioning his habitual close grip on his emotions. Hawkes whispered:

"Look at their eyes. They've got the spirit, by Jove,"

The men's eyes were rolling, showing much white; the eyes that Africans show alike when they are afraid or when they "smell blood." Thick lips, straining apart over big white teeth, showed that these men were not being afraid. They were out to hunt. Whether their game were men or feral beasts they were eager.

"A little up-wind, of course, Barounggo." King said.

Hawkes, remembering some of the rules of hunting feral beasts in India, thought to offer a quick objection.

"Not up-wind, old man; their dogs will smell us and give the whole show away."

King could still grin. "You wanted to plan a strategy of attack. Here's the only strategy. Rush 'em from up-wind and set fire to the first huts. Their own women and brats barging around will raise a confusion that's worth a hundred men."

THE MASAI picked his way, as cautious as a hunting leopard, up the ravine slope. So far the good luck of surprise had been with the raiders. But it was expecting too much of fate to hope that such should last.

The Masai was close to the lip of the ledge on which the village nestled, when footsteps slip-slopped along a path. Bovinely heavy-eyed, a scrawny, quite naked black man stumbled along the path. A brute-jawed lout, it was easy to picture him howling delight at a fellow human's torture.

The Masai was at the very edge of the path, his great bulk only half concealed by a bush. The other raiders were close in a straggly line, deploying to jump the lip of the ledge as best they could. Every man's breath froze on the intake.

The tribesman saw none of them. Dull-eyed, he shuffled on. Breaths let go softly. The Masai, moving like a huge cat, rose up in the path behind him and drew back his arm with the great spear blade on a level with his own ear.

A magnificent shape of destruction, he might have been an out-size copy of the javelin thrower done in black granite.

But then the Masai changed his mind. Nobody in Africa knew better than he that it was difficult to spear a man so suddenly dead that there would be no last shriek.

Softly he stooped to lay his spear on the ground and then his legs bunched ready under him; with a short, rushing bound, like a lion springs on an ox, he launched himself at the man.

One great hand clapped over the fellow's mouth, the other found his middle. The man flung arms and legs wide, but not a sound came from his throat. The Masai's lower handhold slid down the man's body to his thighs, and he spread his legs, while his toes searched for a grip on the ground.

He set himself, and then the watching men could see the

power of the great fellow swelling into the muscles of his shoulders and back.

Like, M'fumbuli, the great earth spirit of his own savage mythology, he heaved on the man's face and thighs, his own knee in the victim's back; and as M'fumbuli draws force from the earth through his toe tips, the power swelled bigger and knottier into the Masai's muscles. The black boy's limbs writhed hideously; there was a crunching crack, and they writhed no more.

The Masai straightened up and threw the body over the path's steep edge.

"*Whau!*" his deep voice growled. "That one, perhaps, is one who chased my honor from me the other night."

Over his kill he forgot the need for silence. The body rolled chunkily down the ravine side with a clatter of stones and debris.

A boy's face appeared over the edge of the higher shelf to see what occasioned the noise. It took perceptible seconds for the thought to impinge upon his brain that here was death. Then he yelled shrilly and his face disappeared.

Hawkes' hoarse shout was on his heels. "Mark away! Over the top, men!"

THE RUSH of men was after him, yelling now, as Africans must. Straggling bamboo huts were before them. All the dogs in Africa seemed to be there, yelling defiance. Sleepy men were ducking out from low doorways, lurching back to grab up spears.

One fellow, less sleepy then the rest, stood before the huts. The Masai, running as well as ever he bragged, outstripped his own racing mob. The fellow lunged a spear at him. The Masai twisted his stomach aside and drove his great spear like a lancer. A foot of the blade stood out behind the fellow's back.

"Ss-ghee!" The Masai hissed his imitation of a spear entering meat and bone. His impetus twisted the fellow round like a top, dragged out the blade, and he raced on.

The raiding mob yelled for blood behind him. It was King

who retained presence of mind to stop and set fire to the first
hut.

King saw little of that fight. His whole energy was applied
to fighting his own way through to find the largest hut in the
most favoured location; it, he knew, would house that blood-
lusty young ju-ju doctor chief. He fought through a scrambling,
howling free-for-all. Black bodies weaving, white eyeballs
staring, arms waving, and the whole of Africa yelling.

He passed Hawkes and his twin native constables, all three
kneeling with their backs to the wall of a hut. He yelled, "Come
on! Get the chief! Nail him to a tree with a spear through his
chest, and the rest'll run."

They didn't hear him. They knelt in admirable discipline and
fired precise volleys.

King fought on, yelling. The fires he had started fought
behind him, roaring and eating up bamboo and thatch.

He found his hut. It was unmistakable. Apart, a thing of
mystery and blood, fenced with the clap-trappery of the craft
and skull-topped poles.

"If only he's still skulking in there!" King grated hoarsely;
and in the same moment, looking at the blackness of the low
door, he half hoped that the man might not be there. There was
no time for thought. He dived for the opening and squirmed
as he rolled, grabbing wide into the dimness for standing legs.

The air swished. An axe head chunked into the hard-stamped
earth floor. Missed him! His hands found legs and heaved at
them. A bulky body sprawled down on him. Together they
rolled. The axe head swished again. King caught an arm. A hand
caught his wrist. They rolled. Teeth bit into his neck, like a dog
ape's gnawing for the jugular vein. King smashed a fist on its
ear. It yelled, splutteringly through a full mouth, and the teeth
let go. They rolled.

"The brute's as strong as a gorilla!"

At dusty dim intervals King could see black silhouettes

ducking out through the beehive doorway—women, ululating shrill news of death within.

Not yet. But all to the good, King knew furiously, for the demoralization of the brute's people. The fight was a struggle to determine whether the axe would break free first, or the pistol butt.

As strong as a young gorilla, and with teeth to help. But King had the white man's weapon that the African never understands. At furious intervals he had a spare fist. At furious intervals it hit something.

The axe fell somewhere. The brute howled and pushed away to struggle to its feet. King with it. They wrestled furiously. Clawing hands on King's throat. Big teeth gibbering close to his face. His own hands were on the brute's throat.

They whirled. King's back crashed against the central roof pole of the hut. It felt like a broken spine. King whirled away from it, swinging to retaliate for the maneuver. The brute's head crashed against the pole. Its yelp was a groan and its big body shuddered.

A fury of victory surged through King. Ruthless.

"That much for Ogilvie!" His breath hissed through a bitten lip. Like a hammer thrower, stiff-armed, he whirled his body again and aimed the brute's head at the post.

"You did it, you swine!" The brute's ear thudded squashily on the post and it shuddered enormously.

"You tortured him!" Again King battered the lolling head against the post.

"You burned the grand big heart out of him!" And once more, with all of King's strength at full arm swing. The brute's head went limp on its thick neck and it sounded like a bag of broken crockery.

AND THEN King knew that the choking smokiness of the hut was not kicked dust but fire roaring in the thatch.

He lurched out into the sunlight; and there were men, his

own men running frantically about, looking for him. Hawkes, too, bleeding but alive.

"Great Scott, old man!" Hawkes had the trained unemotionalism of the British soldier in victory. "You look like you'd been in a dog fight! You're bitten like— Come, let's get out of these blazing huts. We were thinking you must be down somewhere."

Sanity was coming back to King. "Where's Barounggo and the Hottentot?"

"I saw them around. Come on to a cool spot beyond the village. By golly, what a strafing we gave 'em!"

Beyond the village limits, where the fire would not reach, the Hottentot was binding gashed men with whatever bits of dirty cloth he could find. The Masai appeared, smeared with blood as though he had been painted with it. None of it seemed to be his own. He reported:

"Four of my *askaris* have fought their last fight with much honor. Death is a little thing and is better than life such as these."

He pushed forward two abject things, Ogilvie's servants, yammering still with the terror of the death from which they had been rescued.

The two constables were scratched up, as was Hawkes, but nothing serious.

"Discipline." Hawkes pointed the moral to King.

"Yeah. But I'll bet you my boys got more notches to their spears." King looked back bitterly on the burning village. "That's what hurts 'em. Burn up their pots and blankets; that hurts 'em more'n some dead men."

The rescued servants still groveled in their terror. Among men who had fought and killed and still licked their wounds, they were objects almost of disgust. King could see that Hawkes thought the same.

"Not worth my good four," he told Hawkes. "But—British subjects."

"Yes," Hawkes affirmed soberly. "And must be protected."

King only growled.

"Well," Hawkes said, "it's done. Let's collect prisoners and go."

"Ah! Prisoners!" King turned to the Masai. "What prisoners are there, Barounggo?"

The Masai tapped snuff from a little horn that he carried in his ear lobe and sniffed it hugely. "For myself, *Bwana*," he said, "the fight was too fast to stop and tie up prisoners. I shall ask my *askaris* whether any man fought so poorly as to catch a prisoner."

A little farther down the ledge was the place of the sacrifice. The crude cross still stood, awaiting its next offering. One of the servants screamed.

King, his face set in a hard mask, plowed his boots through the cold ashes, kicking up a cloud of smothering dust. Out of it, expressionless, he picked a charred skull and stared at it. Then methodically he set to wrapping it in his handkerchief.

"Good Lord, old man." Hawkes was shocked at his apparent callousness. "What d'you want that thing for? We have all the evidence we need, with these two men as witnesses."

"The hell with your witnesses," King snarled at him. He finished wrapping the skull, and he very nearly fooled Hawkes with the hardness of his tone.

"I'm no ethnologist. But, looking at it, I'd say this was Ogilvie." He strode on. "And still the job wasn't good enough." He scowled a last bitter look at the smoke of the village, a black plume against the sun. "Come ahead. Let's go."

HE STALKED ahead in silence, fast with long plunging strides. It was not till they were away out on the plain that he was done with his brooding and he shook his black mood from him. Not till he came to the rounded boulder beside which he had once before stopped for a breathing spell. He waited till the rest came up with him, and he was grinning.

"These rocks," he told Hawkes. "About the African geology that I told you you'd become interested in. This long line of 'em at every five miles. It wasn't inflexible glaciers. It was Britishers. Brought 'em here in trucks. They mean, in big loud tones on both sides of 'em, 'No Trespassing'."

Hawkes stared at him before the significance of it soaked in.

"You mean—" His jaw dropped.

King grinned shamelessly.

"Yeh. It's the border line of your empire. Where we've been is Italian Ethiopia."

"But— But, good God, man, international boundaries, these days, are—"

"Yeah," King laughed at him. "So you said about me, coming over."

"But— My sacred word! This constitutes an armed raid into the territory of a sovereign power! And the Italians are so—"

"Yeh, the Italians are so— And you British are so—" King's laughter left him and he was brusquely fierce. "Listen, Britisher. Suppose you'd known, what would you have done? You'd have reported regretfully to your chief, and your chief would have reported to your Colonial Government, and your Colonial Government would have reported to your Home Government, and where would you have got? And in how many months?"

"Well, but—"

"And this border line is two months' journey from headquarters, on foot! And you had your two sacred British subjects to rescue before this very night! Not that I give a hoot about your subjects. But—" King's rush of words choked down to his grim mood again and he walked on in silence. Slowly then it came through his teeth:

"Those murdering monkeys got Ogilvie, And Ogilvie, I'm telling you, was a whole white man. Worth ten thousand filthy ju-ju devils and ten international complications!"

He stalked on. Hawkes was beginning to appreciate the justification of his action, but the official aspect of it still appalled him. King waited once more for him to catch up, and he was laughing at the anxiety on Hawkes' face.

"Don't worry about international complications. Have common sense and shoot in your report that you rescued your two good subject and punished Ogilvie's murderers and did a job of holding up white man prestige. You don't have to draw a map of the place."

Hawkes could see the glimmerings of an out. Enough, at least, to laugh.

"I'm beginning to understand what those headquarter fellows meant about 'that cunning devil, Kingi Bwana'. You made something of a bally ass of me, leading me into this sort of a mess."

"You'll learn, copper," King said dryly. "Like you learned to do a good job here. And it wasn't me that started it. Friend Mosha— Hey, Barounggo! Did anybody kill Mosha?"

The Masai solemnly drew his thumb diagonally from his left shoulder to his groin. "It was long due, *Bwana,* and our honor was involved."

"Aa-ah! Well, that slick ju-ju doctor sent Mosha to wheedle you into arresting me and snaking me away from here. He knew durn well I shot that elephant on the other side of your No Trespassing sign."

"Oh! You did? Well, my word! What I mean, dashed slimy of the beggar. But now that you remind me of it—" Hawkes was embarrassed and painfully apologetic. "I'm awf'ly sorry, old chap, but I've just go to arrest you for coming over the international line without a passport. Sorry, but—"

King laughed without a worry in the world.

"Inflexible as glaciers. Well, copper, I'm not fighting the British Empire. Ogilvie saved me from an African lion once. I guess, on his account, I can take what the British lion has to hand me."

SLAVES FOR ETHIOPIA

THE RAID was perfectly timed and faultlessly executed. It had to be; otherwise it would never have caught King as completely as it did.

It wasn't King's fault. King was a prisoner—on a basis of parole, it was true, but none the less a prisoner of his British Majesty's East African police, charged with heinous crimes, not the least of which was entering jealous British territory without a passport from over the controversial border of even more jealous new Italian Ethiopia.

Capt. Hawkes, with two native constables, all as ragged and battle-worn as King himself, commanded the might of Empire, So King, with his big Masai henchman and the six that were left of his sturdy spearmen, slept the sleep of the careless in safe and well-policed British territory.

It was then that the raid came. The raid was commanded by Ibn Faraq the Fatherless, with some fifty hellion Arabs as hard-bitten as himself. It was one of those things where fools rush in where angels fear to tread and often enough accomplish what wiser angels would not attempt.

Not that Ibn Faraq was anybody's fool. With the stigma of Fatherless upon his youth he had to be as clever as a devil and as ruthless, to rise to the eminence of best hated slave trader in all southern Arabia. It was just that Faraq didn't know about things and people along the Kenya-Ethiop border.

But that didn't deter Faraq for a minute. Slave raiding over the Ethiop border and then juggling the catch back and forth over the line as pursuit threatened, had been a profitable game for men who were bold enough ever since the border had been argued about.

In the good old days of the Ethiopian regime, nobody on that side of the line cared an awful lot, and dusky Ethiopian *Rases* who had slaves of their own were not averse to a little clandestine connivance, despite the death penalty decreed upon slave trading by their enlightened Haile Selassie.

In those days the game had been easy. But now that Italy was master, things were tightening up, even though the border was still far and roads were not at all. The Hadramaut market offered ever better prices, and every Arab knows that Allah created Africans for the purpose of being slaves.

So Faraq the Fatherless swore by the Prophet's coffin that was suspended in midair in the revered borderline between the empires of men and angels that he would go over and look for himself over this border between the empires of Italy and England, neither one of which he revered at all in these troubled days when men didn't know upon just whom Fate was laying the favorable finger.

When Faraq swore by the coffin he no longer hesitated, for he had much experience about the close connection between vacillation and coffins. So he loaded his fifty good men and fifty good Japanese rifles into his big sailing dhow that was now lying up in one of the creeks behind Port Durnford, and here he was, savage enough at the scarcity of good slave meat to tackle anything—and what matter if a couple of white men slept so carelessly in this wilderness? Faraq had much experience, too, in the technique of night raids. The first thing King knew about it was a muffled yell from a startled police sentry who should have been awake; and before he could swing his legs free of his cot; the tent in which he and Hawkes slept peaceably together collapsed upon them like a net, its ropes cut, and strong arms and legs swarmed all over it, flattening out cots and poles and everything under a smothering blanket of canvas.

King had caught leopards in that kind of trap—strong canvas that fell at a given word upon night creatures nuzzling over bait, and strong men who then rushed out and swarmed all over it. He preferred canvas to a net for the reason that a leopard's claws—or a lion's—might puncture the canvas but couldn't rip it.

Out of the wreck of his smashed camp cot, in pitch blackness and smothered by heavy bodies that swarmed all over the tent, the best that King could do was writhe like a grub in its cocoon till, inch by straining inch, he was able to work a hand down to his hunting knife and stab blindly at lumpy weights that pressed over his face. Somebody yelled in an agonized pitch; hot blood came through the gash in the canvas onto King's face, and then more weights pinned him hopelessly down. Somewhere in the choking blackness of dust close beside him he could hear the angry splutters of outraged imperial dignity.

"By Gad, I— Somebody will smart for—Ugh! Some of these border tribes need a—Oo-oof!—damned good lesson, by Jove."

King saved his breath. He had no illusions about dignity. He knew that people who jumped white men's tents at night were not worrying about anybody's distant retaliation.

His limbs were limp with sheer suffocation before he was dragged from the trap, swathed with ropes, as he had himself many a time dragged a furiously fighting leopard.

FAULTLESSLY EXECUTED. With the exception of the man whom King had stabbed through the canvas, the whole affair had been bloodless. Slave meat was valuable cargo these days. Not like the extravagant days of Tippoo Tib, whose Zanzibari Arabs used to come howling with fire and sword and trade musket into an African village and counted themselves well paid if fifty men out of a hundred lived and lucky if as many as half of those ever reached the market.

...the neck of his lance-head... slid past.

Nowadays a live slave was worth very much more than the free marauder who might have died capturing him.

Even Barounggo, the big Masai, stood trussed, wrist and foot and knee, and the broken haft of his spear twisted the cords behind his back. An Arab was balancing the great blade of it, smiling happily.

"A guard put to this stub of a haft," he was saying. "And this thing will make a fine sword for me."

Faraq the Fatherless was well pleased. He sat on a pile of the white men's hurriedly collected camp gear as on a throne, his elbow on one knee, his fingers clawing gently through his beard in thoughtful appreciation. A long lance leaned against his shoulder. A horseman in his own country, he retained here, where the *tsetse* flies killed off all horses, this symbol of desert manhood.

Torches lit the scene. Black shadows, dingy whites of the Arabs' clothing that billowed ghostly in the night wind, red lights on their Japanese rifles, already rust-spotted. At the outer edge of the torch flare lumpy shadows were already captured slaves, crouched in stolid African apathy. A line that glittered in and out amongst them was a chain to which each man's wrist was handcuffed.

Faraq's heavy-lidded eyes glittered like the metal as he nodded. "These be men worth the catching, not like these scrawny villagers of the last two weeks." The metallic eyes stopped their roving on the Masai; white teeth flashed out underneath them. "That one alone, well tamed and delivered safe in Hadramaut, will pay half the cost of the hunt."

Barounggo saw that the chief spoke of him. He glared back. Fierce in his pride, he growled an announcement that ought to correct this foolish mistake.

"I am Barounggo. *Elmoran* of the Masai. With these six *askaris* I serve the Bwana Kingi."

Faraq lifted an eyebrow at one of his men, who understood Swahili. At the man's translation his smile was wider. "*Yah, Ahmakhat.* Tell the fool that the Kaid of Tefalit will bid as high as two hundred English gold pieces for him."

Barounggo's muscles, already swollen over his cords, bunched so that the lights glinted off them as hard as from the guns. The

Arabs behind him laughed. They had tied many a strong man before this.

Barounggo swallowed down his personal rage for a later reckoning. First to correct this mistake. He knew what was proper. It was not fitting for a white man to announce himself. Let this mad Arab but know who was who, and the thing would be settled with apologies and surely with gifts to pay for indignity; though for himself blood would be the only apology.

"This white man," he announced, "is the *Bwana wa policea* of the *Britisi serkali*."

"And that," Capt. Hawkes told King with an angry satisfaction, "will change the fellow's tune in a hurry."

Faraq the Fatherless only rolled his eyes sourly to rest on the bedraggled majesty of the Law. He looked at the officer without expression and without comment. Barounggo's eyes rolled in wonder. The long-reaching might of British law and order was something that even King didn't buck.

"This one." Barounggo intoned it as a good servant should. "This one is the *Bwana n'kubwa* Kingi, whom all men know. *Mwinda ya ndhovu, na wagasimba, na pigana ngagi na mikonake*, hunter of elephants, slayer of lions, who fights gorillas with his hands." The extravagant titles rolled sonorously forth. "Who shoots and does not miss. Who burns up his enemies. Who—"

"By Jove!" Hawkes was still confident enough to let go a short laugh. "You'd think the colonial police are nothing here. Is the man reciting your deeds or is he just bragging?"

The recital brought response, though not as overwhelming as the Masai had expected. The Arab who knew Swahili and the East African Who's-Who cried out, "*Wah Allah!*" And he told Faraq quickly, "*Har'm*. This one is forbidden. Evil fate comes to those who meddle with him. His name is ill luck."

Faraq, who knew nothing of Africa, said only: "Peace. I am not a fool to hold white men. Nor will anybody buy them in any market. Take the two out and turn them loose. The rest we hold. Away now. Swiftly."

That was the faultless technique of Tippo Tib, whose reputation was that a million slaves had passed through his hands—a
well planned raid, well executed, and away before pursuit could
be organized.

A CHILL dawn, dripping dew as heavy as light rain,
slanted its light on King and the representative of Empire,
crouched under a huge wild fig tree for its protection. Alone in
an empty plain that undulated away to every point of a dusty
yellow horizon; foodless, fireless, weaponless, stripped down to
every last item of any value. The raiders had taken everything
and gone.

Alone as far as human companionship or aid went. Game
was plentiful enough and with an instinct of security that must
have been instilled by the devil they browsed closer than
Hawkes had even seen them. King could have thrown a stone
into a herd of Semmering gazelles.

Utterly alone and utterly forlorn. But King was able to grin
at the police officer. Hawkes was savagely furious. His ruddy
British complexion was blotched white with anger; his fingers
kept twisting his once trim military mustache. It was King's
grin that brake through his control to flare out:

"I suppose you're grinning, you damned Yank, because you
think I won't be able to take you in now. But no fear, my lad, I
will." It was anger and pride speaking. King could have taken
and broken the man over his knee almost as easily as could the
Masai. His hard lips spread a little wider and he settled his big
shoulders back, like into an arm chair, amongst the great flaring
roots of the tree.

"You don't mean that, copper."

"Oh, don't I? By gad, if it takes the whole British army, I'll—"

"Yes, yes, I know." King's level brows went up, half mock-
ingly. "I've heard it all before. But you've forgotten one thing."

"I'll take you in if it's the last thing I do before I have to
resign my job over this disgrace."

"You've forgotten that those filthy pirates have my man Barounggo and six of his men. I can't go with you now—not yet."

Hawkes looked at him as though he had been physically hit, and then his normal redness flushed deeper.

"Sorry, old man. I was talking rattled. A thing like this happening, don't you now. Really awf'ly sorry. Two of my men taken too. But, dash it all, what can we do?"

King's smile hardened.

"Go after 'em," he said simply.

"Of course, old man. Certainly, and all that. But placed as we are—empty-handed, you know—"

"You forgot one more thing."

"What?"

King's eyes narrowed, as though contemplating the not unpleasant prospect of possible action.

"That my other man, the Hottentot, is about due to meet us somewhere along this trail with that new English rifle that you touted so high that I had to send for it."

Hawkes clapped his thigh. "That's true. Splendid! We'll be able to feed ourselves and—" Hawkes' enthusiasm went out cold. "If those bloody bandits don't catch him as he comes along, all unsuspicious."

"Not that one." King's grin went sidewise at Hawkes. "He won't be lying up any place, safe in charge of your British law."

Hawkes took the thrust with a chagrined grimace. "*Mea culpa,* old chap, and you don't have to rub it in. I suppose I'll have to offer my resignation and all that. But anyway, if he comes through—"

His jaws tightened. "We'll be bound to catch a native runner sooner or later and send him in to Todali outpost with a wire for reinforcements, and I'll at least take my men back with me."

"By the time your official reinforcements are organized," King said with conviction, "those fellows will be to hell and gone with no trail behind 'em. That's plain raiding history. You go tag along with your platoon that won't dare cross an international border. Me, I've got to step right after their trails while they're high and going."

"But dammit, old fellow, what can the two of us do against them? Fifty of 'em, well armed."

King grinned at him, almost fondly. "So you would bull-dog along, eh?"

"Well, er—If you're so blasted bent on being crazy, what the deuce else can I do? Though damme if I like it. That business you dragged me into against those juju devils was shivery enough, even with all our men. But two of us! Alone!"

"Us, *and* the Hottentot," King said. "And he'll have his own gun, that military .303 that you insist I must have stolen, since they're not for sale, though I can show you where you can pick up a hundred of 'em. Maybe you'll get a chance to use it and show how well a soldier can shoot. Though I'm hardly figuring on that." He stared hard-eyed into the distance, his mouth a thin crooked line. "It'll all hinge on that new rifle. If it's as good as you say—" He shrugged useless speculation from him till the rifle should come. "Come on. We'll build a high smoke for the Hottentot, and if you must eat, I'll show you how to snatch *mjumbakaka* lizards under the rocks. As good as frogs' legs at time."

CHAPTER II

FOOLS RUSH IN

IT WAS afternoon before King jumped up with a glad "Ha!" A black speck like an ant was crawling over the rounded top of a far *kloof.* "He has made wonderful time; we've that much luck with us."

The Hottentot put on a spurt of sheer bravado and arrived at a trot. A small man, as wizened as a monkey and as wiry, he was dog weary but as cocky as an ape that has performed a good trick. He panted his first complaint.

"This new gun, Bwana—it weighs at least two pounds more than any proper gun should. Carrying it and my own and cartridges has broken my liver. There should have been a camel."

"It was good running, Apeling," King said. "There will be a new blanket with zig-zag stripes, and the extra weight will be equalled in tobacco."

"*Whau! Assant, Bwana.*" The little man wriggled his quite surprised thanks, suddenly abashed at the munificence of the reward that his complaint had craftily played for and that he had never expected to come so easily. "Where is that great oaf Barounggo and his *askaris?* Can I not be absent a few days but that useless fighting man leaves his master in a plight that one would expect of bushmen savages?"

King's lips bit hard and all the angles of his face stood out like strained muscles. Soberly he told the Hottentot about the raid.

"And therefore," he said grimly, "much depends upon this new gun."

The Hottentot's pose of jealousy of his master's other servant's mere brawn was forgotten in quick concern. All his actions were those of an enraged ape. He jumped up and down grimacing with his mobile lips. He threw clods of earth in the direction where the slavers must have gone.

"Then for what do we wait, Bwana?" he chattered. "Let us away. We can raise the tribes against them. Look, Bwana." The little man's mind raced as alertly as a goblin's. "On the Ethiopian side the Has Woilo; for a promise of aid against the Aitalian conquerors, will lend us a hundred of his spearmen who hide in the hills."

"Even that I may do yet," King said without a qualm. "I wait only for this gun. Observe now, Kaffa." His eyes roved far to pick out a suitable mark. "That broad acacia trunk; five hundred yards I guess it, and full five hundred I shall need. Go and hew

me the bark from it at man height, so that the white shows
clear for a space the spread of your two small hands and stand
then clear to signal. But first eat. There are fat lizards in the hot
ashes."

Kaffa spat disdain. "What is food, Bwana, that it should delay
vengeance? A man hunting blood eats when he may, or the day
after that. I go. A space of one hand spread, Bwana, is better
for a sighting. What is five hundred yards to the Bwana Kingi?"

Hawkes looked after the little trotting figure.

"By gad!" he said. "How do you get them that way, my dear
chap? We can't."

King laughed shortly.

"You fellows rule them," was all the explanation he gave. He
took the new rifle from its canvas case. His eyes sparkled over
it like the sun on its fine mechanism. He talked to himself and
it rather than to Hawkes.

"Jeffries magnum .300, eh? The best long range big-game
gun in the world, are you?— Ten pounds without scope, twelve
with. Well, you'll be needing all of that for your power. If you're
as good as you look—" He squatted down on a low termite
mound and scuffed holes for his heels.

Hawkes ventured criticism. "I say, old man. Hadn't you better
take the prone posish to sight at five hundred?"

"Live targets," King grunted at him. "Fifty of 'em, coming
yelling at you with guns that are no old trade junk, don't wait
for you to take prone positions in between getting up and
running."

He snuggled his eye down to the scope and then cocked his
eyebrow over it at Hawkes. "Damn if this thing ain't as good
as any German scope I ever looked through."

It drew Hawkes like a defensive wasp. "Well, rather, my dear
chap."

THE FEEL and balance of the gun chased King's somber
mood from him as though he might have been fondling a

beautiful woman. He grinned at Hawkes' patriotic stuffiness and adjusted the scope to five hundred and snuggled down to it again. The slash of white on the acacia stem looked about as big as a watch. The Hottentot stood appallingly close to it, nonchalantly at ease.

"Damned little fool," King muttered. "He does that just to brag about me. Some day he'll—" But he fired.

The Hottentot took off his loin cloth and stood naked. He waved it in a weird wig-wag system of his own. King grunted and twiddled the micrometer mount.

He fired four times. The Hottentot pranced like a naked imp and wigwagged wildly. King stood up grinning happily.

"You Britishers always did build a good bull gun. So then I guess we're set."

"If you say so. But, er—won't you let me in on a little bit of your mad programme, Yank?"

King's deadly mood came down upon him again.

"Sniping," he told Hawkes grimly. "Ever see the damage and demoralization a good sniper can do? I'll pick 'em off, by God, till they'll talk terms. Harry 'em back and forth over the border; I may even have to enlist with the old rebel Ras Woilo against his new white masters. But I'll get my men back."

Hawkes stared at him.

"I suppose," he mused aloud, "that's how you get 'em to be that way." Then he shrugged. "Well, I'll be having to resign anyway. So—"

They shook hands on it.

King was counting cartridges when Kaffa came back. He whistled tunelessly through his teeth. "Only five packets. Fifty thin rounds! And five of 'em fired on sighting in."

"And fifty raiders with modern rifles." Hawkes gloomily added up the mad prospect.

Kaffa stood on one leg and scratched at his knee with the other, squirming like a monkey on a tight rope. The little man understood English, though he tried never to let on about that.

"What evil is on your mind, Implet?" King demanded.

The Hottentot looked far afield and his little black eyes were inexpressibly mournful.

"Fifty," he said, "was all that that Inglesi shopkeeper would deliver with the gun, saying that he required to keep the balance for other such guns. Therefore, Bwana," He brought his scratching foot down and stood ready to jump. "Knowing that Bwana must have a need, or he would never have sent me for the gun, it came into my mind to steal two packages." He produced from his meager loin cloth two flat packets of shells.

"Whee!" King whooped. "Twenty more shots!" And then he forced his expression down to seriousness. "For that, little devil's spawn, this hidebound policeman will put you in jail; or at least will fine you much money after restitution is made. But, for this once, I will myself pay it."

"By gad!" Hawkes was as ill at ease as the Hottentot. "I suppose I'll have to lag him. Clean up the job and all that before I resign. But the fine is on me. Really, old fellow, I insist."

King cuddled the extra cartridges.

"Maybe," he said, "you won't have to resign. Still an' all, sixty-five shots allows all too little for misses. Guess we'll have to live on lizard meat."

Hawkes twisted his raggy mustache to its best semblance of good form.

"Good enough grub for the last few meals of three crazy men," he said.

THE NEXT day's sun was beginning to throw long shadows before them when Kaffa pointed silently to the sky. King considered the birds wheeling in high watchfulness.

"Ha! Not anything dead, or they'd be dropping. Not game, that high. Men."

"And camped," the Hottentot supplemented, "or the birds would not be so many. And who but a slave train would camp this early?"

"Come on," said King through his teeth. "Edge over to that hill."

He said nothing more till they crouched on the hill's top and looked over the plain to a straggle of men under a group of far mimosa trees. Then he said, more as a statement than a question.

"You Britishers got an old law, haven't you, that a slaver can be shot on sight?" The distant men, hard black and white in the direct sun, looked like little penguins.

"Why, er—I don't know. I—"

"You pulled it on the old blackbirders often enough. What d'you figure the distance?"

Hawkes judged it with military precision. "Seven hundred, I'd say. But, dammit man, you're not going to try from here? Out in the open hilltop like this? They'll rush us like howling dervishes. And no defensive works."

"Majuba Hill," King told him laconically.

"By Gad! Were you at Majuba? But you couldn't have been, what?"

"Before my time." King was kicking heel holes for himself. "But from all the telling, there were some Boer Africanders dug no trenches at Majuba; only defense was clean shooting." He was shuffling his buttocks into the stiff grass. "And the best they had was old Mannlichers, nor any scopes, either." He clicked the scope up to the seven hundred. "And the light is perfect, smack on our back, and the wind dropping to nothing for sundown."

The Hottentot stood as motionless as a well trained caddie, awaiting the drive. In a low monotone he said; "That tall fellow, *Bwana,* who stands clear of the tree there."

Hawkes fidgeted with the rifle that he had taken from Kaffa. He drew the bolt, made sure that he had five in the magazine, pushed one into the chamber, sighted in the direction of the far mob.

"Crazy Yankee blighter," he kept grumbling.

King turned one sardonic eye on him. "Better hold it till

they're into two-fifty. Those open army sights are something sinful on shells beyond. And if we can't stop 'em then, I hope you can run just a leetle faster'n them. You know any prayers?"

He brought his eye down to the scope. His teeth clicked together with the soft cluck of the set trigger. His breath held tight and he pressed the last fraction.

The tall fellow who stood out alone just disappeared into the knee-high grass.

"Oh, shooting!" Hawkes breathed. "Shooting indeed!" Just as though commending a grand play at cricket.

There is—and unfortunately so—an astounding callousness that descends upon men after they have once justified to themselves the need of taking human life.

There was no more question in King's or the police officer's mind as to the propriety of their lone-handed war than there was in the Hottentot's.

"Hell!" King grunted. "I've seen even soldiers score a stationary target at a thousand. But it won't be so easy now."

Thin cries floated back to them and men scurried as aimlessly as ants. In the tenseness of waiting even the Hottentot was whispering. "They have not seen yet whence came the death. Look, there stands another one staring."

King fired again. That one disappeared into the grass.

"Spotted us now, by golly!" His tight grin was on his face as though painted on a robot of steel and wires. "Here they come."

MEN STREAMED out from the camp, yelling, waving guns. There must have been full thirty of them, every one fiercely bent on achieving the honor of annihilating the three on the hill. Some stood long enough to fire aimlessly.

"Dopes!" King fired again. His words formed themselves in his throat rather than on his lips. "They'll learn to run zig-zag before we're through." He fired. "And near half a mile is a lot of running in stiff grass." He fired again. "Ha! Atta gun!

Hundred percent so far. Whites o' their eyes, hell. But—" Again. "They got guts."

With merciless method he picked the foremost runners so that those behind could see them drop. But they kept coming, yelling hoarsely. Bullets began to kick dust and to buzz like wind-driven hornets. King was not ashamed to duck after each near one had passed, but he held grimly to his position.

Hawkes cursed him.

"One lucky hundred and eighty grains is all they need, chum." But with obstinate pride he sat stiffly upright alongside of King and made a point of it to expose himself every bit as high.

The Hottentot had no traditions of national pride. He lay as flat as a beetle. King's words, his cheek distorted hard against the butt comb, came as a hissing jumble. "Try your luck, soldier. It's stop 'em now or run like hell." And then, "Whoopee! They're winded and down to a walk."

Hawkes began to shoot. King was too furiously busy to look, but mechanically he kept grunting: "Watch shells. No ammunition train behind us."

Suddenly the Hottentot leaped high and waved his arms. The men below them were dropping to the grass for cover from the murderous accuracy of the fire from the hill. King snatched out a hand to the Hottentot's ankle and jerked him sprawling.

"Monkey head!" A bullet passed. "Whit!"

"By George, we've got 'em!" Hawkes laughed with the cracked exultation of men in the hot surge of battle. "We've got 'em. They've no cover!"

From their eminence they could look down on the shadowed depressions in the tall grass. Hawkes dropped to the regulation prone position and picked out his targets. King grunted and followed suit. Lying down, the Arabs were shooting closer than even a madman could afford to deride. The furious speed of King's movements settled down to cold method.

"Whoever runs now won't be us, by God. Allow to shoot just over the grass tips, and it ought to get 'em in mid-spine."

*The slave column, like a long black
snake, staggered away.*

A few hot seconds ago it had been yelling figures full of furious life that disappeared every now and then into the long grass. Now, every now and then a yelling figure lurched out of its shadowed depression and dropped back to make a new sprawled shape.

It takes hard disciplined troops to stand that sort of thing—troops of the sort that had died in their thousands and stuck to it and finally won the murderous hill of Majuba. These slave raiders were not of that breed.

Somewhere out of the grass a man wailed. "*Wah Allah kerim!*" for God's mercy and protection, and jumped up in a frenzied dash for the camp.

Hawkes whooped and let go. The man curled like a rabbit and rolled for yards.

That was the break of panic. One after another, and then in a yelling mob, the Arabs jumped and raced for their lives, each frantic not to be the hindmost; and behind them came the devilish bullets, smashing at their backs.

King sat up and fondled his rifle like a lover, only his words were not at all romantic. He said in plain hard American: "That's learned the dogs some."

Hawkes was breathing normally again. He paid King the highest compliment he knew.

"By God, sir! You should have been a soldier. Your selection of position and tactics was masterly."

King turned and peered through his rifle barrel into the low sun before he grinned complete satisfaction at what he saw and said: "God forbid. I may get my tough sledding against your damned officialdom, but I'm my own boss." He looked down over the late skirmish ground, now in the shadow of the hill, and grinned out wide. "I'm a trader. Come on, Kaffa."

"What mad thing now?" Hawkes had to know.

"Rifles." King said curtly. "You soldiers leave 'em on the battlefield. Not me. There's no government buying mine. Should be about twenty scattered around—and cartridge belts. Sun smack in their eyes, we're safe as bugs in a Kavirondo blanket."

The official in Hawkes rose to protest. "You can't trade rifles in British East."

"Copper," King laughed at him, "You'll never know where I trade 'em." And darkly he added: "I may have to trade with rebel Ras Woilo if I can't win my boys back any other way."

"But—Dammit, man." Hawkes' whole credo was violated. "You can't do that—arm natives, you know, against white Italian rule."

"Yeah," King snarled, "and the Arabs are brown and my Masai and his boys are black. But they're *my* boys! Get it?"

"By gad!" Hawkes breathed. "Yes, I think I see. You still should have been a soldier."

"C'mon," King said roughly. "I got to get those rifles and find a cache for 'em before the lions come around. An' then we'll have to hustle us up a good roost in a tree."

Later, examining those good Japanese guns, he shook his head. "Pity. These cartridges and all. Damn, if it wasn't for lions we could annoy those fellows a whole lot all night."

FARAQ THE FATHERLESS was no fool. Lions, he knew, could be a menace to a few men at night, but not to a caravan. In the darkness he silently folded up his tents and slipped away from under rifle range of that accursed hill.

With daylight King didn't even bother to go up and scout. He looked for circling vultures and laughed. "African spotter planes. And there'll be other hills behind 'em, and three good men can always outwalk a caravan. C'mon, let's hunt lizards."

There was an element of the terrifying in that remorseless pursuit. If not for the fear it engendered in the raiders, it would have been ludicrous—a raiding army running before three. Not that those fierce Arabs would ever had admitted they were running. But Ibn Faraq cursed savagely and judged it wise to make for safety with what winnings he had. True, slaves were worth twice as much as free guards, and his slaves had remained immune; but if he should lose many more of his guards, there could still be naked spearmen by the way who would lash themselves with howling and drums to a frenzy of retaliation.

So Faraq lashed his slaves with whips and blows to make the best speed that could be beaten out of them. And King laughed grimly and presently topped a hill behind them.

Moving men with their slender height were of course more difficult to hit than moving game at the same distance, but King's sniping remained deadly. He didn't hesitate to lie down now in the prone position for long range shooting.

"None of 'em fool enough to try rushing us again, is my bet. And even soldiers can target at a thousand feet, shooting this way. Hell, I'll even call the shot."

The Hottentot, like a top grade caddie called it. "That one with the black cloak, *Bwana;* he will be a chief."

The black cloak lurched forward before its owner ever heard a shot. The three could see a furious scurrying along the length of the black line that was slave meat, could see arms rise and fall, knew that the arms held whips.

The column drew out of range. Men milled behind it in a confusion of distant yelling. King risked a long shot at running game. The Hottentot clucked querulous disapproval. King only laughed in short barks. There would be still other hills in a three weeks journey between here and the coast. A lot could happen in three weeks.

It could happen, of course, to either side. And Faraq the Fatherless had not attained his rank through any fatalist habit of letting Kismet do whatever it would to him. Faraq drew some of his men together and harangued them.

It was the Hottentot whose monkey alertness first spotted Faraq's manipulation of Kismet. When they next caught sight of the caravan it was well out of range; but Kaffa, whose eyes had never been ruined by education, peered at it under his hand and then gave of the education that he knew.

"Bwana, the dust that they made rises not so high. Therefore it is in my mind that they travel not so fast."

"Ha! Getting tired out." Hawkes said.

"And Bwana, they pass close to that hill ahead of us, which a wise man must to do; yet it is in my mind that Arabi surely have learned to be a foolish thing chief is surely not a fool."

"By Jove! I wonder what's ahead. Maybe a war party."

"Not ahead. It is in my mind that the men who walk are fewer in number; yet we have not slain so many."

"Aha!" King stopped dead. "Little wise ape, there will be two blankets and enough tobacco to buy a little ape woman. Not a fool, surely, is our slaver."

Hawkes did not as yet get the Hottentot's devious reasoning. "What's the delay?"

"Ambush," King whispered. "Waitin' for us right along the track we'll take for that perfect sniping hill. So we just won't. We'll circle, and maybe we'll spot something from that *kopje*. Bet they'll be lying up in that patch of *nyika* grass."

THEY WERE. A dozen of them, lying in wait with the crafty vengefulness of buffalo. When a flanking fire broke on them from the hill that they had never suspected they fired no shot in return. They bleated and ran like woolly sheep, their

billowing *jellabahs* marking them out against the yellow grass
for the slaughter.

"Apeling," King told the Hottentot, when he dared waste no
more cartridges on the range, "there will be two women and
the price of a cow."

The next high ground showed the caravan headed due north
and hurrying like haartebeeste harried by lions. King looked
from the distant scurrying figures, and his mouth twisted hard
with a disappointment that was none the easier to take for all
that he knew it had been bound to come.

"Here's where you're through, Britisher," he growled. "They're
working the old trick of heading for the holy Italian border line
that you dassent cross without your permits and your passports
and all your mess of official red tape. Guess it's a lone hand for
me from now on."

Hawkes watched the slave train go and his frown echoed,
showed the struggle of the ingrained law-abidingness in him.
His shoulders jerked in a short shrug.

"I'm through anyhow." His anger flared out. "And damn your
eyes, Yank, don't you forget there's two of my own men there
whom I dashed well will take back or stay here with 'em."

King reached a long hand to the other's shoulder and shook
it.

"There's times," he said, "when I think a soldier is pretty near
as good as a free man—even a British soldier."

"Come on," Hawkes said brusquely. "We can get another pot
shot or two in before dark."

The Hottentot let it slip once again that he understood,
though he pretended that he spoke only out of his observation;
and as always, he shrouded his words with the circumlocutions
of native thought.

"It is in my mind, *Bwana,* that the Bwana Mwewe, in his
eagerness for slaughter, has forgotten *mwewe's* wisdom."

Mwewe meant hawk, so the Bwana Mwewe was as inevitable as though so designated by his sponsors at his baptism.

"What now, Little Wise Ape?" King was never so cocksure as to pass up anybody's advice. "And let it not be an impertinence just because a little wisdom has newly earned you a cow."

"Nay, *Bwana*, no impertinence." The little goblin stared with solemn eyes. "Who in all this land would offer an impertinence to a *bwana* of the *policea*, when even the *mkubwa* Kingi shows him respect—without fail?" He remained carefully just out of King's reach. King, out of the corner of his eye knew it. So the Hottentot went on to expound his observation. "Only it is in my mind that when *mwewe* is hot in the hunting, the quail hurry to cover beneath the bushes; whereupon *mwewe*, being wise, hides behind a tree; and when the birds, feeling themselves safe, emerge to fluff their feathers in the dust of security, *mwewe* swoops to great slaughter."

"By jove!" Hawkes' military mind grasped the simile quicker than did King. "The fellow is right. Bring up the artillery when the enemy thinks he's safe over the line. Biff 'em when they're bivouacked for breakfast. Demoralize 'em no end. By gad, I'll buy the boy another cow!"

CHAPTER III

LAST STAND

THE DEMORALIZATION that Hawkes predicted was as complete as anybody could have hoped. Bivouacked the slave raiders were. For breakfast, for rest, for surcease from that relentless harrying against which their only retaliation was impotent rage.

At the edge of a water hole they sprawled, under trees. Careless smoke went up from cooking fires. Safe. Over the border— well over it, where there could be no doubt about international lines, where the governing headquarters were a month's journey away and where foreign officialdom dared not follow.

A perfect spot, such as slave raiders had picked throughout the long years.

When the first man suddenly pitched on his face over his own cooking fire and a full second later the far pop of report came, there followed a full five seconds of unbelieving silence. Then men scuttled for cover, throwing dust from their heels like veritable quail. A full second later their screams floated back on the morning breeze.

A bold few, enraged to desperation, started a half-hearted charge towards the hill. They could see nothing with the sun in their eyes; but there was a hill and from it the sniping must come. So they charged, yelling, brandishing guns.

But first one man dropped, and then another, and the charge broke up and streamed back to the water hole, where there were trees with fat trunks behind which to shelter.

"They've learned," King breathed.

Frantic whips rose and fell. The slave column, like a long black snake, writhed into broken movement and staggered away. White draped figures straggled after them, northwards, away from that deadly range. Fires remained burning; pots remained over them; lumpy bundles remained on the ground.

Kaffa scurried over the deserted camp with all the inquisitive ardor of a baboon turning over rocks for grubs. He came to report with as much glee as one that had found a locust colony.

"Loot is here, Bwana; four good daggers and seven cloaks that smell bad and a sack of wheat meal and cooked food in the pots which they will not have had time to poison. Only the meat that scents the air is that man whose face fell into his own fire."

"Pah!" Hawkes grimaced. "I had been thinking of venison." But his instinct was to turn to the strategic values of things. He was exultant. "Victory, by Jove. Victory with captured commissariat."

King remained dourly dissatisfied.

"This is coming too easy," he said. "Africa isn't that kind. That slaver devil will be dealing some hell out of the deck yet." Savagery bit through his voice. "And he still has our men. Let's eat and on."

THE NEXT hill showed how sorely the relentless sniping had taxed the raiders. A little straggle of men was walking across the plain—plodding slowly and openly on the back trail.

King jerked his shoulder to throw off his rifle sling with an expert movement that slapped the gun into his hands.

"What fancy trick now?" he wondered.

But Kaffa hopped on one leg in excitement and said: "*Bwana,* that tall fellow amongst them who walks like a stork, nobody could be so ungainly but our Bukadi; and that other who leads with his head low, that one is surely Ngoma, the trail smeller— and they come unbound, as free men."

"Eight of them." Hawkes' voice broke high in its tenseness. "Capitulation, by gad! Return of prisoners."

King's voice was hoarse. "What of Barounggo, little ape? Do you make him out?"

The Hottentot stopped hopping. He peered under his hand. "Nay, *Bwana,* that great oaf I do not see." His voice was anxious. "And his form surely would stand out from the rest." He tried to be optimistic about it. "Perhaps he follows with a message."

King walked the hill top with long strides; his scowl was deep cut in his face.

The men plodded to the hill top. Two of them came to attention and saluted Hawkes. The other six said, "*Jambo Bwana.*" But there was no big-toothed grin of greeting on their faces.

"What of Barounggo?" King snapped at them.

Ngoma, the trail leader, reported: "*Bwana,* that man who has no name, having no father, said: 'In the name of Allah let there be peace'. And he said, 'Tell those white men,'—and he cursed you in the name of many devils—'tell them that no man who has fallen into my hands has ever escaped alive. Yet I do what I have never done. I return eight of those whom I have taken'."

"What of Barounggo?" King snapped again.

"Barounggo, *Bwana,* is alive, though beaten with many whips; for one who beat him came too close and Barounggo, his hands being chained, smote him with his foot and that man died on the second day in great torment."

"What of Barounggo?" King thundered at them.

"Barounggo he holds, saying that his price alone will pay the cost of his losses. Therefore, he says, let there now be peace, lest a worse thing happens."

"Peace?" It exploded from King. "While he holds Baroung-go? I'll—" His shout choked down to a small dry question. "What did he mean, lest a worse thing happen?"

"That we do not know, *Bwana.* He is an evil man and his rage is like a trapped leopard's."

"By God, if he—" King took a huge breath to hold back futile threats. His men shuffled uneasily before him; it was not their fault, of course, that their great Masai leader was not with them; but they felt as privates must who have accepted liberty while their officers have been held.

The lines of King's scowl remained just as deep, but the shape of them began to change to his thin, hard-lipped grin. He said:

"All right, you men. There will be a running for this day and this night and the next day. Kaffa knows where rifles are hidden. With them you will be men once more."

Kaffa jumped high and screamed his sudden exultation. The men stood and stared like oxen with white rolling eyes till the significance of it broke on their slower minds. Then they shouted their cavernous African laughter.

"Give us but a bellyful of meat, *Bwana,* and we run for a week of days and nights. Free men we are, but our manhood remains bound in the iron chain of those Arabi dogs who eat women's food. Give us meat as we are accustomed and we run for the slaying."

"By gad!" Hawkes murmured. "If we could put that spirit into a regiment!"

King's grin broke sardonically on him. "You heard what they said? Free men. They don't fight on order from far away politicians. This is their own grudge fight."

Hawkes frowned at that blasphemous philosophy, but he didn't argue.

"With weapons," he said, "you'll have a small army."

"*I'll* have?" King's cold stare matched Hawkes' frown. "What about you? You've got your two back."

Hawkes turned to his two men, his voice crisp.

"T'shun," he told them. "Take orders. You two will go with these men. What this little Hottentot commands, you will obey."

The two saluted. King laughed at the gaping men.

"All right, Kaffa," he said. "Away. You have a *Jaipani* rifle. Feed the men well. By tomorrow's falling sun we expect you to catch up with us. We shall leave a well marked trail, so that there may be no delay."

Kaffa laughed. "Nay, *Bwana*—what need of a trail? Not a man here but will smell his way back to the vengeance."

KING AND Hawkes squatted alone on a hilltop that King had warily chosen with the sun at their backs. Hawkes frowned down at the slave raider encampment, a mile away.

"The blighter is getting clever. Plenty of trees for cover and a good water hole. Dashed good defensive position."

King's eyes ranged over the hazy landscape. He cocked one eyebrow at a far herd of galloping zebra.

"Scented lions," he commented without interest. "Probably lying up in that *donga* waiting for supper time." With a little greater interest he pushed his chin towards a thin plume of smoke above the foothills to the North. "Probably Ras Woilo's rebel guerillas waking up to the doings over the border."

"Ras Woilo!" Hawkes' interest was much greater than King's. "Ha! Then we have 'em. The Ethiops harryin' 'em from that side, and our own fellows ought to be along this evening with those rifles."

King shook his head. While his big Masai remained a prisoner his experience of Africa could conjure up a hundred dev-
iltries.

"Not that easy, soldier; not in Africa. And the Ethiop can't
change his habits any more'n his skin. It'll take 'em a week to
get organized anyway; and what's more, if Woilo cuts in, there'll
be complications—like rifles, and your damned official conscience. It was all you could stretch to come over the border
into foreign territory. If I have to make a deal with Woilo, rifles
for help, you'll kick like an eight gauge full choked." The grin
came sourly though. "Besides, I'm a trader. I don't want to have
to lose the good couple dozen rifles I've won to date. We'll play
our own hand—yet a while."

But Hawkes remained full of optimism. "There'll be eleven
of us. Eleven men with white leadership have won a province
in Africa before now." But the precariousness of the empty
wilderness injected its note. "If nothing stops our fellows from
getting back."

That was one point on which King had no fears. "Not around
here, nothing will. Not those boys, with what they've got on
their mind."

Nothing did. Though darkness had come and King's pessi-
mism about African mischance was crowding down on Hawkes
before King said; "Ha! Hear 'em?"

All that Hawkes could hear was the hoarse snuffling of a
brace of hyaenas.

"That'll be them." King said. "The brutes following along
their flank, hoping for someone to drop dead." On the farther
side of the hill, away from the scattered glows of the encampment, he built a small fire. And in another half hour dark forms
emerged into its light.

"We would have been here sooner, *Bwana*," the Hottentot
reported, "only that the lions were unexpectedly many and the
game therefore few and far, and these great louts demanded
meat for their running like empty baskets that have stood idle

"Couldn't expect to—
guess this one!"

till the ants have eaten their bottom out. Six and twenty rifles, *Bwana;* not a one lost; only a porcupine had found one hiding place and eaten up three good cartridge belts."

Hawkes chuckled. "Twenty-six! I hadn't realized our sniping had got so many of 'em—I should say, your sniping, old man."

"It was a good running," said King. "There will be gifts for each man."

"It was nothing, *Bwana,*" the long-legged Bukadi boasted. "When a man's belly is full, what is a little travel? We be ready to go as far again."

"That's good," King said dryly. "Come then and look the other side of this hill."

The men stumbled after King to where a view of the further plain showed pin points of fire. Angry growls came at the reminder of their shameful captivity.

"So have they always camped in their security. *Whau!* Let us fall upon them, *Bwana*, while they are fat with sleep."

King shook his head, slowly, regretfully. "Not that easy. Give 'em a chance, and those men can fight like devils. There's not enough of us to take that kind of a chance. But the crowd of us together can maybe spoil their beauty rest some."

Hawkes saw the immediate military value. "Those johnnies have slept in peace all these nights while we've been roosting in trees. We've never dared to make a thorn *boma* against beasts for fear they'd send out a scouting party and find it. A little of this night medicine ought to jolly well bring 'em to talk terms."

"Come ahead," King said shortly. "Keep together. Who straggles will be lion meat."

It was when they could distinguish dim forms amongst the fires that King halted his party. "One good thing, we know that the slave chain isn't being coddled by any fires." He gave his simple instructions to his men. "Shoot, drop immediately flat, and crawl two hundred yards. So, if they charge out into the darkness, we be somewhere else." And he grunted with a grim vindictiveness: "Show these jaspers something about night raids."

THE PLAN was as perfect as Faraq the Fatherless One's original raid and as faultlessly executed. The fusillade that crashed out of the empty darkness was answered by seconds of stunned silence; then came yells that were more startled than fierce, and scattered shots stabbed vindictive tongues in the vague direction of the darkness that was as empty as it had been before. Those African *askaris* knew things about crawling through high grass that Arabs could never understand. Bullets flew futilely over where the raiders had been, and the raiders were belly flat and well away from there.

Well and thoroughly away before King halted them again. Not much could be distinguished of the camp; fires still glowed, but no indolent forms were in their light.

"I don't know that this nets us any score," King said. "Maybe your two policemen can shoot in the dark, but my boys are spearmen; they couldn't hit a hill in broad daylight. But it's morale we're aiming at more than men. Ready, everybody? Shoot when I do, and away again."

Somebody must have hit something, for a shriek came that was more than just rage or fear. King laughed. Bullets came where he had been, but nobody showed a head. It takes a peculiar kind of courage for men to charge out into a blackness where guns might be waiting.

Round at the farther side of the water hole King called another halt for another volley. Hawkes was jubilant. "This is the technique, my boy. Nothing like night sniping to smash morale. I've seen even our own men raw and ragged after a night's persistent attention by Waziri tribesmen up in our Afghan frontier."

"It's too easy." King remained obstinately pessimistic. "You're talking about an organized army that can afford to lose a few hundred men. We can't afford to lose one. We're too blamed vulnerable. Anything happens to me, and what then?"

It was not complimentary, but Hawkes knew well enough that only King's craft and experience had put life into their amazing campaign. He said nothing. King grumbled on: "These Arabs aren't anybody's fool. Give 'em time to think, and they'll hatch out a devilish idea or two for reprisal."

A little later he was able to point to proof of his foreboding. It happened on the farther side of the water hole, out in the direction from where they had first fired into the camp. A chillingly brief and admonitory drama of the African night.

Just three short sounds. The harsh, *waugh, waugh,* of a lion and a single hoarse shriek. That was all.

"What was it?" Hawkes whispered. "What happened there?"

King barked a short laugh. "Somebody hatched an idea that didn't work only because he didn't know Africa." He let the Hottentot translate the tragedy. "And how do you read that, little Apeling?"

Kaffa moaned the crooning noise of a frightened monkey. In itself it had an eerie sound, coming disembodied out of the blackness into which he merged. "I read it, *Bwana,* that a man crept out to lie in wait where we might return; but the lion found him first."

"A *wahabi,*" Hawkes breathed. "I've seen 'em do it before."

"What's a *wahabi?*"

"These Mohammedan johnnies. Some fellow's rage will drive him fanatic and he'll take oath on his knife blade to go out and get an enemy or die."

"Well, that one died," King said. "But they'll be hatching other things. Ready, *w'askari?* Another volley and keep up the merry game. Yet let no fool become careless."

T H E   G A M E might have gone on all through the deadly night, but that Faraq the Fatherless, desperately gathering his wits in between the sporadic volleys, proved King's contention that he was nobody's fool. A voice called out from the blackness of the camp, where all fires had now been smothered.

"Give ear, white men," it shouted. "Give ear and consider. We lie behind a barricade of iron and meat. A rope of slaves surrounds us. Chained two deep they sit. Shoot them, if you will. Those that die will still sit, wedged between their fellows." And another voice laughed like a devil assured of many souls.

"So!" It hissed from King. "That's one good one they've hatched. This was too easy to last. Nothing to do but get back to our hill before daylight. Let 'em catch us on the open plain, and we're cooked."

It was on their own safe hill that the next good idea hatched. They were almost at the summit, walking at their ease, when a rifle spat out of the darkness. King heard a smack beside him like mud spattering on a wall, a strangled grunt from Hawkes, whose dark bulk lurched up against him.

"Get him!" King roared. He snatched at Hawkes' sagging form. The other dark shapes were already roaring response and rushing forward. The rifle spat again. The ground thudded under racing naked feet. King lifted Hawkes and plowed on for the top. Beyond him the pack of fierce voices bayed on the quest, casting criss-cross over the hill's dome, till one yelled the find and all the others converged in chorus to be in on the kill. Blows thumped dully; steel-shod rifle butts clacked together in their eagerness; a voice yelled horribly above the roaring of furious men.

The Hottentot loomed close out of the dark. "The man is pulp, *Bwana*. What of the *Bwana Policea?*"

"A fire! Quick!" King ordered. "Below the brow, where they can't see it."

Hawkes' voice came, shaky but game. "Another *wahabi*, by gad. And that one got through."

King was cursing himself in a fury of profane self blame.

"Couldn't expect to—guess this one." Hawkes offered comfort.

"It's out-guessing the other fellow that keeps me alive in Africa," King said savagely. "Quick with that fire, Kaffa. Where are you hit?"

"Left shoulder. But I'll be—all right, old man. I've—stopped 'em before now."

The sputtering fire began to show up a smudge on Hawkes' coat.

"A knife, Kaffa!" King swore again. "Thank Pete we got this much." He sawed at the coat and the shirt beneath it. There was only one hole, and that was bad. An emergent hole on the other side, however torn, would have given King less anxiety.

He made a pad of the material he had sawed out, yanked out his own shirt tail and ripped it to strips.

"You've stopped 'em," he said through tight bitten teeth, "where you've had a hospital corps behind you." He set to bandaging the pad in place with his ripped shirt tail.

"If those swine hadn't looted everything in my kit I could do an amateur job on you with the boys holding you down." He cursed the inadequacy of the shirt tail and tore out his shirt front. "Iodine, anyway. This isn't so easy. Not even a canteen of water nor a blasted thing to carry any in." He tied the crude bandage tight. "Stop bleeding, anyhow. There. We'll have to get you down to water. Means open plain in daylight—wide open to have 'em rush us. Hell! What a gaudy mess!"

Hawkes felt that he had to apologize. "Sorry, old man, and all that sort of thing."

King stalked back and forth, swearing. This smashed his every plan. His savage temper at the contumacy of Africa broke from him in explosive bursts. "I knew it. It was coming too easy. Now, by God, we're stymied."

Hawkes felt soldierly embarrassed.

"I'll be all right, old man," he insisted weakly.

King never believed in belittling danger just for the comfort it might offer.

"Don't fool yourself, feller. You'll be a lot worse before you'll be better. This is Africa. Heat, dirt, bugs—and not even a pellet of quinine. You can't fool with that sort of thing. I'll have to rush you in to where you can get some attention."

"Oh, but I say, old man!" Hawkes suddenly understood the reason for King's impotent fury. "You can't do that. Your Masai. They've still got him."

"Think I don't know it?" Helpless, King set to pacing the ground again. It was maddening, how far reaching could be the results of a simple wound where the ordinary aids of civilization were not at hand, how out of all proportion to its intrinsic damage. After a fury of pacing King stopped and looked down at Hawkes' dim form in long silence.

"Really, old fellow," Hawkes assured him, "I'm feeling quite chipper. I'll do all right till you get your man back."

King's voice softened.

"You've got your guts, soldier. But wait till the sun gets up tomorrow. Wait till it begins to inflame. Fever, festering, gangrene. I've seen 'em all happen."

"Perhaps," Hawkes said hopefully, "something will turn up tomorrow."

But his eyes were bleak.

BUT SOMETHING did turn up in the morning. A man called excitedly from the lip of the hill: "Men come from the camp, *Bwana*. Not for war. They carry a flag of white cloth."

King snatched up his rifle and ran to look. From the top he called back to Hawkes, "Two of 'em. With a burnous tied on a pole."

"By Gad!" Hawkes was still well enough to get up and totter to see for himself. He was there before King, intent on the approaching figures, knew it. King growled at him.

"Pulling the old bulldog stuff, eh? Don't forget, soldier, every move you make will pile a degree onto your temperature."

"Gad!" was Hawkes' only response. "A flag of truce! I jolly well knew that last night would knock an awful hole in their morale. A delegation to talk terms, by Jove."

"Talk something, sure enough. But I see nothing to crow about yet." King's eyes narrowed on the two men; and as they came closer his eyes widened to stare.

It was no mere delegation; it was Ibn Faraq in person. Tall and darkly vindictive, he stood and stared at King, leaning on his long desert lance from which the dingy rag of burnous fluttered. His eyes, bloodshot with barely controlled rage, moved from King to the group of men behind him. Their fierce mutterings affected him not at all. His eyes passed on to rest on

Hawkes. Their expression changed no whit from their scowl of hate. His lips moved, but his anger made his sonorous Arabic tremble. His fury at his own lack of control exploded from him in a harsh grunt that his interpreter understood.

"The *Djeeb al Rais* says," the man translated, "that he has made here the only mistake in all his career; that he has learned now many things about the *Bwana* Kingi. He believes that your word given is given and stands good."

"Surrender and asking terms," Hawkes said. "Don't grant any."

"Not that easy." King's morose frown of the last two days was giving place to the hard-mouthed grin that faced impending action. To the interpreter he said: "*Ataka nini?* So what?"

"He has learned that you set great store by the Masai; that you value him more than all these men who were returned free, and that therefore, rather than the peace that was offered, you risk further fight—and wounds." The interpreter's eyes dropped to Hawkes' shoulder.

"*Ataka nini?*"

"Therefore the chief says, if you will give your word to the bargain, he will fight you for the liberty of that one man against the liberty of all these men. If you win, your man is yours and your word will be to go in peace. If he wins, he takes these and goes in peace. Man to man, hand to hand, the chief offers to fight you for this stake as men fight."

"Oh, I say!" Hawkes ejaculated. "What I mean, that's a bit thick!"

King still grinned. "Why should I fight for what is mine to take?" And he bluffed. He pointed to the thin smoke columns in the far hills. "The Ras Woilo has my messages and is already on his way with at least a hundred men."

Ibn Faraq barked instructions.

"He says, 'I have observed, and therefore I come this early morning to offer this bargain.'"

King grinned and shrugged, and the Arab barked again.

"And he says, 'If the *Bwana* Kingi is afraid to fight for this stake that I offer as a man, to win or to lose, one thing at least is certain. By the Sacred Coffin I will surely slay that Masai before the Ras Woilo comes."

The grin jerked out of King's face. He stared under knit brows at the Arab. Faraq the Fatherless stared unblinkingly back. There was no doubt that he would carry out his threat. A captured slave meant only a certain money profit to him. King turned slowly and stared at his men behind him. They stared back like oxen, uneasy and silent, their eyes rolling white while they knew that King deliberated their fate. King's eyes dropped from them to Hawkes.

The Arab barked again behind him.

"He says," came the interpreter's voice, "'Only I do not want the white man. He may sit where he is, or he may crawl, or he may fly. His fate will be in the hands of Allah, who is sometimes merciful.'"

"Don't consider me in this thing, old chap," Hawkes said, as though talking about some sporting proposition.

KING SCOWLED on into the ruthless responsibility that was being thrust upon him. Lives hung on not only what he would decide to do, but how well he could do it. He swung back to the interpreter, his shoulders hunched forward as though he were already in a fight.

"Tell him, yes, I'm a whole lot afraid, and for a whole lot of things. And tell him that I can make no bargain for these men. They are free men, not slaves. But for myself, I will make a bargain. I will fight him for my Masai alone. If he wins and if he can thereafter take these men again, their fate is in their own hands."

A barely perceptible smile flicked across Ibn Faraq's face before his quick, growled acceptance.

"He says, 'I agree to that bargain. Provided that the fight is as men fight—man to man, with lance and knife.'"

"Good Lord!" Hawkes pulled himself to his feet. "Don't do

it! Man, that's an awful chance to take. His own weapons, and—"

"Have I any other choice?" King snarled a question that needed no answer. "I've got to get you to a doctor, starting now—slung in a hammock on a bamboo pole. What kind of a chance would we have in open ground—with their merry turn to do the sniping?"

He swung back to glower at Ibn Faraq's complacent confidence.

"Tell him I'll call his play. Man to man, like he says. Only tell the devil I have learned nothing about him or his word but evil, and even if I trusted him I wouldn't trust his other devils. Therefore I add this to the bargain. Let him bring the Masai, alive and free, to stand as the stake for which we fight; and let him bring not more than ten of his men to watch the fight is fair; and I'll fight him for that stake, with any tool he likes— lance or knife or empty hands and teeth."

Ibn Faraq's saturnine smile came all the way out.

"*Mas-Allah!*" he exclaimed.

King knew that common Arabic expression. Praise be to God.

"He says," the interpreter added, "'I will be here within the half hour.'" Ibn Faraq smiled upon King once more and turned to go.

"And tell him," King shouted after them, "to bring a spear— the Masai's spear. I don't trust any weapon of his."

A silence came down on the hill like the silence that had gripped the slavers' camp when bullets came out of the night. Hawkes broke into it.

"Good Lord, man! You've allowed him the choice of his own weapons. The fellow is a lancer by his long training. You should have—"

"Swell chance I had of anything else. D'you know how many shells I got left? Just six!" There was a grim little joker there that King could suddenly laugh at. Now that the thing was done, the heady recklessness of men who are ready to fight settled on him, and with it came the bare-toothed grin of fighting men.

"You said it. He's a lancer, a soldier on a horse. He's got no horse here, and all that his weapon has is length. I've lived on my own two feet and kept out of the way of things for a long time."

"And you pretend you never take a chance." Hawkes could see no humor in any of it. "Crazy Yank!"

CHAPTER IV

"MAN TO MAN IT IS!"

WELL WITHIN the half hour a cluster of figures emerged out of the shade around the water hole and headed for the hill. There was nothing hesitant about them, nor anything serious; they came, rather, as to an exhibition. The wind brought bursts of laughter that replied to jests.

"Pretty damn sure of things, huh?" King's eyes narrowed, as he saw a burly figure amongst them that was certainly no Arab.

The Hottentot hopped on alternate feet, but his little round eyes were as sad as a chimpanzee's looking out on the world's inexplicable mysteries. He pleaded pathetically, as for the boon of a banana.

"*Bwana*, the word of white men is a god that we do not understand. Let that god's anger be on me who have no gods. Give me but permission to shoot at him as he comes near. With six shots out of one of his own Jaipani rifles I might surely hit him before he could run out of range. Moreover, *Bwana*, how can one man give a word for another? I have given no word."

King laughed at him. "A fine casuist school you have studied, Implet." But his laugh turned ruefully to Hawkes. "Not the first time in Africa that silly civilized inhibitions leave the white man out on the limb."

Hawkes shifted his position on the ground and winced. "And that," he said grimly, "is the real white man's burden."

The Hottentot stared mournfully at them.

The gang came to a straggling halt. Boisterous, unruly, their open lips and wild eyes showed excitement, but no anxiety; they jostled each other and laughed at their own jokes.

"The bounder has brought the toughest ten of his gang," Hawkes said gloomily.

King laughed. "Figures to take nine of us back."

Only Faraq the Fatherless stood unsmiling amongst his men. His dark temperament, unlike a white man's, was settling down to surly rage for the vengeance to hand.

King's grin on him was ugly. "The bargain was that the Masai should stand free as the stake for this fight."

Ibn Faraq lifted one satanic eyebrow to his interpreter. The gang opened up. A man cut the ropes that were biting into the Masai's arms.

"The man is a mad bull," the interpreter said.

The Masai dropped to his knees before King and put his great arms round King's thighs; he bent his forehead to touch his master's waist. King could see on his naked back the raised welts, as thick as a finger, of hippo hide whips. The Masai's voice vibrated deep.

"Do not do this thing for me, *Bwana.* The man is a spearman and has a devil besides; and what does *Bwana* know of spear play or of devils?"

King put his hand on the big fellow's shoulder. His voice was unnecessarily rough.

"Up, old warrior! Have we not seen blood together before now? And what insult is this? Have I not seen enough of your spear play to have learned something?"

"*Aie, Bwana!* But it was much blood of other people and little of ours." The Masai straightened up and worked his big shoulders, tentatively, as though uncertain whether they were free. "*Hau, Bwana!* I breathe the first whole man's breath in

"We have seen blood before, Bwana!"

many days." His submissiveness became the fiercely eager challenge of an *Elmoran* who has had the hot bravado to go out alone with shield and spear and slay his lion.

"*Bwana,* make another bargain with this Fatherless One. Let me but put haft to my spear and let me fight this hunter of men and his ten while *Bwana* stands free and applauds the slaughter."

The man stood superb in the sun, black as old iron, his great muscles throwing blacker shadows on his naked skin. King shrugged wryly. "Barounggo, old Blood-Letter, I'm afraid this clever Arab thinks he has a better bargain than that."

"Then, *Bwana,* if he will be afraid of such an offer, let him take me and go in peace to his own country, according to his own offer. I will yet escape and devastate the land."

What King did was a very undignified thing for a white man

in Africa. He reached his hand to grip the Masai's shoulder and give it a little shake. But he spoke to him as an African can understand.

"Braggart," he derided. "Must we listen to your boastings all day? Go rather and cut a straight branch to fit your spear—not too long, and heavy in the butt, as who knows better than yourself. Go swiftly, for the *Bwana Policea's* wound must not sit in the sun."

FARAQ THE FATHERLESS stood and scowled through all this delay. His face was masked black with hate. King grinned hardily back at him.

It began to be apparent that the white man's cheerful recklessness was more disconcerting than the Arab's ferocious scowl. The boisterous confidence of Faraq's lowers began to ebb from them; their faces darkened and their loud voices fell to low mutterings. On the other hand, King's *askaris* began to grin sheepishly.

"*Kefule!*" the lanky Bukadi suddenly guffawed aloud. "What has been this fear of ours? Barounggo is here and the *Bwana* is here. It is well. Let us sit and watch."

The Hottentot shrilled at them. "And forget not that I, too, am here. Oxen that ye be without the wit of the lice in your heads. Wisdom it is and not brawn that accounts for any of you being here at all."

"When the monkey is contented," Bukadi said, "the leopard must indeed have lost his claws." The men hunkered down, as callously content as for a cock fight.

The Masai came back. His great three feet of spear blade was fitted to a stout pole, peeled white, barely longer than the blade itself. He balanced it critically in his hand. His dark face seemed to be satisfied, but he had a complaint.

"A fair balance, *Bwana,* and with a good weight to push the stab home. But the steel spike for the butt end was lost by these desert baboons, who know not what makes a good spear."

King took and hefted the thing. It must have weighed all of

seven or eight pounds. "The hell with an iron spike." He spoke more to himself than to the Masai. "A good thick butt with honest weight to it would suit me all the better." He turned to grin, hard eyed, at Ibn Faraq.

"All right, guy," he said in English. "Man to man it is."

It came to Hawkes suddenly that he had been thinking that the Masai's savage menace was something stupendous as he shouted his challenge. But he saw King now as physically hard and as grimly competent a fighting man as all his military experience had ever known.

King remembered a last detail. "All men stand back twenty paces, and the agreement is that no man interferes."

"By Jove, I'll see to that—Kaffa, bring me a rifle." Hawkes pushed himself to a sitting position. "I can shoot one-handed at this range. I'll dashed well see that nobody interferes."

Ibn Faraq threw off his burnous. He was every bit as tall as King, a lean, stringy man. With his long lance he could outreach King by a good half length.

The Masai gave soft advice.

"The body sways inside of the foolish point, *Bwana,* and the Masai blade then slashes up from groin to chin."

Ibn Faraq didn't grin, but his eyes contrived to glitter through his scowl. He held his lance as a horse lancer should, under his right arm.

"Aa-ah!" It rasped from King. "That's what I'd hoped." He held the Masai spear as Barounggo never in his life did—with both hands wide apart, slanted across his body.

Hawkes let out a whoop. "I knew it! The bayonet stance, by Jove! I knew you must have been a soldier!"

IBN FARAQ showed a surprising agility in a sudden leap forward and a vicious thrust, swift and straight at King's chest. The neck of his lance clicked against King's haft, between his widespread hands, and slid past.

"Now!" Barounggo roared. "Now to rush in and rip the bowels from him."

But King was not quite familiar enough with the weapon to have been that fast. He circled warily on light feet, suddenly enormously confident in his ability to fend off a savage point by the method evolved by white men, even though the instrument was not precisely a white man's. He grinned out of the corner of his mouth toward Hawkes.

"Wrong, buddy. Never a soldier, but—" He fended another furious thrust, and this time lunged full arm with his point. It fell just short of the Arab's throat. "Hell! Another couple inches and I'd 'a' nailed him." He found time to flash a look at Hawkes.

"—But I've played around with soldiers here and there, and some of 'em pretty near persuaded me that a bayonet was better'n a spear—Ha!" He clicked aside a long thrust. "Overreach that way again, and I get you."

He was out of reach, cat-footing round for an opening. "Met some good men amongst soldiers—even Britishers."

Ibn Faraq's rage at the unexpected resistance to what he had counted a sure thing exploded in incoherent blasts of speech.

The interpreter's voice was shaky with apprehension. "He says, men talk less and fight more."

King deliberately grinned at the man's fury. Ibn Faraq replied with the worst insult he knew. He spat at King's face. Truer than his furious spear thrusts, it got home. King's eyes blinked. Faraq shouted and drove with all his weight and reach for King's body.

By a miracle of luck King was able to sway inside of the point before the lance rattled along his defending haft. King grunted with effort as he swung the butt up and forward. It crunched full onto Faraq's mouth.

Had it been a rifle butt, it would have smashed the man's face in. As it was, Faraq this time spat teeth.

His men clapped their hands to their own mouths in their racial gesture of astound. Howls of delight came from the *askaris.* Barounggo roared advice. King could distinguish out of the uproar only Hawkes' restrained and distinctive, "Go-oo-od shot, old man."

Ibn Faraq's rage, while it hampered his thinking, did not deprive him of the ingrained technique of spear and knife. King, of course, had given no further thought to the knife provision of the terms of this duel; but Faraq's dagger was in his sash. With his left hand he drew it and held it flat along his palm.

The Hottentot's shrill yelp came. "*Similia jumbia, Bwana!* He is a thrower!"

A N D   A T that moment Faraq saw his chance and threw, a swift underhand fling for the belly. King, cat-footed, was able to snatch his stomach aside, but it left him hideously off balance. Faraq roared triumph and lunged full length. The lance point flicked through King's leather belt like through wet paper. King felt a searing fire streak along his ribs; in a fractional second that lasted a year he felt the point push through his skin again somewhere farther back and felt wood rasp along bone.

Faraq roared again and lurched forward, his spear in both hands, shoving it on and grunting with the effort of each heave.

King's hands on his spear were all wrong for any kind of a thrust at the oncoming enemy. They had slipped together at the neck of the blade; the haft hung in his hands like a club.

He used it like a club. As Faraq lurched in, he swung it in a desperate arc. It cracked hard over Faraq's ear.

Faraq staggered and went down. But he still held his lance; lying prone as he was on his back, he tugged to free it. Its very length impeded its withdrawal; but the leverage of it, fast through King's clothing and side, twisted King excruciatingly this way and that.

Until suddenly Faraq's own struggles twisted King directly alongside of himself. King heaved up his spear with both hands and drove down at him. The great blade slipped through his chest and back and two feet into the ground beyond.

Faraq's last fury croaked from his throat in great strangled heaves. Impaled like a noxious beetle on a pin, his arms and legs flung out in spasmodic jerks and his back arched mightily to free itself from the earth to which it was nailed. Then blood began slowly to push out around the blade.

"*Whau!*" The Masai's great shout broke the silence. His *askaris* leaped forward, solicitous all together to support King. Hawkes, who should have been lying down, was with them, pawing at King with both hands, one of which ought to have been in a sling.

King pushed them testily from him. "What the hell! Stand off, you gorillas! It's only through the skin—I think." He tried to break out of the press, but the lance, grotesquely horizontal in his side, held him as in a yoke. "Get this blasted thing out." He tugged at it himself, but pressure of skin and clothing held it hideously fast.

"Away, cattle! Away!" Barounggo knew much about spears and their handling. "A spear through meat is no new thing. A knife here!" Like sharpening a giant pencil, he cut through the shaft. "Hold fast, *Bwana*. Just while a man may wink one eye." He gave a jerk. It twisted King agonizingly around. He was not ashamed to yell. But the thing was out.

Barounggo ran the knife through coat and shirt and kneeled to peer through the flap. With expert callousness he poked an unsanitary thumb at the bleeding gash in King's side and followed the ribs around to the other hole eight inches farther back.

"Skin and some meat," he announced. "It is nothing. It bleeds. We have seen blood before, *Bwana*. It was a good fight, though shamefully inexpert. I must give *Bwana* some lessons with the spear."

King was aware of Faraq's ten picked ruffians slowly moving away. They went backward, their eyes bulging at the incredible things that were happening. Barounggo's great arm was around King, offering support. King pushed from him. Those men must not see any weakness.

"As far as your camp you have safe conduct," he called after them. "Such was the bargain. After that follows vengeance." He grinned hardily at Hawkes. "Tit for tat, soldier. I'll have to have your shirt tail for a bandage."

He was talking to avert fuss over himself, and nobody knew it better than Hawkes. So Hawkes laughed weakly, a little hysterical with reaction and rising temperature.

"Now I have to take you in to a doctor," he said.

"Yeah?" King remained unnecessarily tough. "We'll see who takes whom—and I think I can eat. This thing came in the way of breakfast. Hurry, Kaffa. Fast travel is before us."

WHILE THEY ate, King gave instructions. "The vengeance must follow fast, Barounggo, before those raiders may reach the coast. How many are left?"

"But twenty-four men, *Bwana*. It was a shooting that melted men's liver." The Masai breathed hugely through distended nostrils. "Ow, *Bwana!* I smell the killing afar. Swift it will be, for many dishonors mark my shoulders to be washed clean in men's blood."

King's eyes wrinkled in a brief and utterly callous satisfaction. "Good. I can leave you only four men. Four I must have for hammock porters, for who knows, I may myself be sick. You will have to raise the herdsmen of Bunwelo to cut the raiders off, for they will surely flee across the border again from Ras Woilo."

"Surely, *Bwana,* the spearmen of Bunwelo will delay these dogs while I cut them down. But *Bwana* does not come? It will be a merry killing, and this wound is but a spear hole such as we have seen many a time."

King's smile moved quizzically to his lips.

"I am a prisoner of the *Bwana Policea* here for crimes against the British Empire that he has yet to prove. So is Kaffa, for the heinous matter of stealing cartridges that have gone to saving the lives of two constables of the policea."

"Oh I say, old man!" Hawkes shuffled as uneasily as did the

Hottentot. "I can't— What I mean, old fellow—come to think of it, I don't know that I can prove anything; you're so bally evasive. But I suppose I'll have to go through with the regulations—sort of keep the record clean before I resign."

King's smiled grinned at him wide open. "Come to think of it, soldier-copper, you won't have to resign. You don't know what's been going on, nor yet where you are; you're delirious." He amended grimly, "Take it from me, fella, with that bullet in your shoulder and the kind of travel that's ahead of us, you will be good and plenty off your head by the time I get you in—if either of us gets in."

"I'm afraid so. It's beginning to throb already. But my official report—"

"By the time you'll be well enough to make any official report, fella, the newspapers will have made it for you. I'm just a ruffianly trader that you were sent out to pinch. I've got no official conscience to keep me from lying to your sacred government, and to the papers, like every lowdown trader always lies. The report will be that you've cleaned up a slave raid gang and turned loose a hundred slaves. You're too sick to know which side of the border, and you'll never be able to prove t'ain't so. Time I'm through, you'll get promotion."

"Really, old man." Hawkes was shocked at blasphemy against sacrosanct institutions. "I can't allow—I mean, damn it, you do it all and what do you get out of it? Only official trouble."

King laughed. "I've had it before. And I've already got what I'm going to get." He inhaled deep satisfaction and grimaced as he clapped his hand to his side. "I've got my men back." And he pointed a hard brown finger on Hawkes' chest. "I repeat, I'm a trader. I get, besides, fifty good rifles, and you'll never be able to prove where I'll sell 'em."

"Oh, come now, my dear fellow. I can't—I mean, you're a crazy Yank and all that sort of thing, and you don't understand our official code. But you can't mean to tell me—"

"Is that hammock ready, Kaffa?" King called. "Hurry it along. We got a sick man here. He's raving."

CAPTAIN HAWKES of the British East African police pleaded with his prisoner.

"Really, old chap, you must help me out here. You've got to go out and get this brute, whatever it is; catch it, shoot it, or something. Dash it all, the thing is terrorizing the town. Doors locked, children kept indoors and all that sort of thing. The Colonial Government can't allow that."

"Nothing doing." King lounged his length comfortably in his captor's longest cane chair and tinkled a swizzle stick in a tall whisky peg. "I'm a wounded man with a spear hole in my side. I'm scared of mysterious monsters that howl around towns at night where no monsters should be. Besides, I'm under arrest here for not saying my prayers to your sacred Colonial Government."

"You are not." Capt. Hawkes' face flushed. "What I mean, old man, I wired it all to the commissioner and he said I'd better turn you loose on your own cognizance."

"Bet you didn't tell him all the truth." King grinned shamelessly. "Did you tell him about ivory poaching, and that passport business, and that crucified man I shot right before your eyes, and all the other hide-bound laws of yours that you say I've busted wide?"

"I did indeed. 'Pon my word I told him everything, and he wired back—his very words: 'I know that Yankee reprobate better than you do. He's too smart to let any charges stick.' And he said to give you his strictly unofficial regards."

King's straight sandy brows arched. "Yes, I suppose with your staunch official integrity you confessed everything.—And your grub here seemed so good after the two of us living on lizards."

The quite unusual condition between captor and prisoner should be explained by the fact that Capt. Hawkes, new to the district, had set forth, full of indignant zeal, to arrest Kingi Bwana of the backlands for a long list of heinous offenses against His Imperial Majesty's Colonial Government, and in the ensuing skirmishings King had at least twice pulled the officer out of serious holes.

"Awf'ly sorry, old man." Hawkes was apologetic. "I can't extend hospitality any further—officially, of course. And anyhow—" He turned on King with the righteous peeve of a man being let down by a friend—"you've *got* to help me out again. Dash it, if I weren't wounded worse than you, if I could move my shoulder at all, I wouldn't ask you. But—"

"Can't." King said positively. "Can't do a thing without Kaffa, my Hottentot. You've still got him on his confession of stealing those cartridges that saved all our lives. Can't wriggle out of your stuffy law by just recanting his confession."

Hawkes' face darkened to the inevitability of British justice. Then it cleared. "I'll release him in your charge. I can do that on my own authority. I'll have to bring his case up, of course, but I'll recommend a fine instead of jail, and I'll pay it myself."

King grinned.

"Yeah, you would bull-dog it. In my country we'd just get some crook to squash the case and save a lotta everybody's time. Well, I'm an invalid, but since you'll agree to turn my man loose, I'll listen. Just what is this mysterious monster?"

"Hanged if we know, old man. Nobody knows. It's just been there the last two nights, howling and crashing along the jungle fringe. The natives come white-eyed and say it's a ghost gorilla."

"Any killings?"

The Masai, with the supurb skill of a bullfighter,
lunged in and upward with his spear.

"Not yet. But you know how suddenly killing can come in Africa. And our policy, of course, has always been prevention rather than retribution."

Hawkes spoke with serious conviction. King's grunt was ribald.

"Atta boy! Colonial Empire speaking from its pyramid of bones—All right, Britisher, we'll argue it later. We got a ghost gorilla on our hands right now, due to do some murder any minute. Which doesn't make sense, since there's no gorillas any

nearer than your farthest borders this side of Belgian Kari-simbi. Another of those African impossibilities that always end up sticky red anyhow. Okay, then. If that's the price on my Hottentot, gimme a deed on him, free and clear, and I'll stagger forth."

Hawkes, having gained his official point, suddenly became human again and showed his private anxiety. "You're sure you're well enough, old chap? What I mean, fast enough to get out of anything's way?"

King shrugged. "Who knows how much is 'enough' in the jungle? Anyway, I can shoot fast if I can't run fast."

WITH THE lowering dark, three shadows moved as si-lently as shadows should through the deeper shadows that an early moon accentuated along the jungle fringe. King was unmistakable; tall and lean muscled, dressed in British shorts and the hot but practical woolen puttees up to his knees as a precaution against snake bite, topped by a dilapidated shooting coat that gave easy play to wide shoulders; under his arm a rifle that could shoot, at close quarters from that position as straight and much faster than most men from the shoulder.

The shadow that bulked behind him was as tall and even broader, dressed, in the dimness, apparently in nothing at all but monkey garters at knee and elbow and a Masai spear, the blade of which glittered a good three feet long when the moonlight glanced on it.

A pair formidable enough to venture at night into African shadows where a something howled. The third shadow was as grotesquely stunted as the other two were big, a gnome of the gnarled tree root hollows. Despite the heat, a wisp of ragged blanket fluttered from his shoulders as he scuttled behind, before, all around, as alertly as an eager hound, chattering an incessant whisper of comment, advice, caution.

"Pss-sst, Apeling," King told him. "Use your bat ears and nose more and your tongue less. We don't know what this thing may be or how it may attack. That *shenzi* whom we questioned said it was the shape of a gorilla, only it ran with the speed of an ostrich."

"That *shenzi*," The Hottentot scoffed, "was more frightened and foolish than a calfless cow. Men of the plains, *shenzies,* are like these Masai—all things of the jungle are ghosts to them."

"The reason—" The Masai quoted the plainsmen's proverb—"why there are no more Hottentots is because their children are monkeys."

"Of which," King commented dryly. "I wish I could be as certain myself. Less chatter and more attention. What new evil may happen in the jungle not even a Hottentot knows."

Shadows melted in again with shadows, the wavering hands of blind men before their faces, feeling the ground with their feet before setting weight on them, with infinite caution working against the hot night wind.

Until out of a black nothing the Hottentot's voice came. "*Ngalia, Bwana!* Look out. A something moves in the wind before us."

Neither King nor the Masai could detect a thing other than the normal sounds of the night jungle around a peaceful white settlement—the rustle of a porcupine in the dry *magongo* leaves that are impervious to moisture and a curse to hunters, the far cough of a leopard, and the querulous complaint of sleepy monkeys.

The big Masai shook himself so that the quill fringes of his garters rattled.

"So do the ghosts talk to one another," he said uneasily.

King heard a long sniffing noise at his side and he knew that the Hottentot's wide nostrils flared and twitched like a chimpanzee's.

"But the smell on the wind. *Bwana,* is not the smell of '*ngagi* the great ape, whose smell is the smell of an unwashed bushman and carries far."

King ran his coat sleeve over the hand grips of his rifle to wipe slippery sweat from them. "What kind of a smell, then, must we expect?"

"The smell of a meat eater, *Bwana.* Yet it travels with too much noise for the great cats, and it travels, not like cats, but along the cattle trails."

"Assuredly, then, a ghost," the Masai mumbled.

"Sure fits with nothing else," King growled.

Then both he and the Masai heard the thing. A *pad, pad,* of heavy trotting feet and the swish of branches that swung back into place. Then the sounds stopped. The whole jungle stopped still. All the night creatures, disturbed by the unfamiliar something, crouched and held their breath until they should judge it safe to resume their various occupations.

"Looking for us." The Hottentot's whisper came from a

height already above King's shoulder. "Here is a better place to wait, *Bwana,* than upon the ground."

THE MASAI'S pride forbade that he should do anything that his master would not. Only he admitted, "I like this not, *Bwana.* Give me daylight and open ground, and I will meet this thing, foot to foot, spear to spear. But this hunting of jungle ghosts is no work for a man."

Out of the farther silence a rapid drumming sound began to grow, a hollow beating of fists on a barrel chest, and then a hoarse roar that emptied giant lungs as though steam pressure actuated them, winding away in an eldritch screech.

"*Whau! 'Ngagi!*" There was enormous relief in the Masai's voice.

But King remained puzzled and wary. "Not so easy as all that, old warrior. Gorillas don't run at night; they sleep like men. Nor can we smell him. Nor does one howl like that."

The Masai reverted to his superstition. "Then surely the ghost of one that runs and slays by night."

One canny rule that King knew for all dealings with natives was, whatever he might be feeling himself, never to show indecision. He took the direct road of action now.

"Come ahead, you two. If this thing travels the cattle trail, the thing to do is find the trail and wait there. Whatever it is, a two-twenty magnum bullet will stop it."

Masai and Hottentot moaned, but with superb loyalty both followed. The Hottentot even scuttled ahead.

"Careful, little one," King whispered. "Better stay to heel."

But the little man only said: "Nay, *Bwana,* who but I will smell out the cattle path? And who will find the tree that I must swiftly climb when it comes?"

And sure enough, out of the heavy blackness he presently whispered, "Here cattle have passed, as even a Masai may feel with his great toes; the path is wide, as we know by no branches to our hand; and there is a patch of moonlight where the ghost, if it can be seen, must pass. This is a good place from which I, in a tree, can give notice of its coming."

But he did not have to give notice. The monstrous roar shivered in the air again and then the heavy *pad, pad* of feet, not fifty feet from them, beyond a black tangle of jungle.

The Masai's quills rattled and the smooth hiss of his hands passed along his spear shaft. Only a ghost would see those motionless shadows in the shadow.

The sounds grew closer, slanting towards them. The Hottentot's voice came like a bat's squeak from above.

"A path converges into this one, *Bwana*." And then, in the lowest possible range of human sound: "There, *Bwana!* In the trail! At forty paces'"

King sensed, rather than saw a bulk in the farther blackness. He could hear its heavy breathing as it stood and looked up and down the path. He knew that a great formless head swung this way and that by the hoarse hiss of wind between its teeth.

It was a sharp warning to him to hold his own breath, and with that he felt that the thing would not fail to hear the hammering of his heart. His rifle inched forward. Not much to shoot at, a sound, a ghost that bulked indiscernible in the dark.

And then even that sound stopped. The thing must be holding its own breath. It must have sensed, if not seen, something in the blackness. King reached out a hand to find the Masai. By finger pressure alone he tried to convey the impossible message that he wanted the flashlight directed straight ahead, that with the pressing of the button he would shoot.

A leaf that crackled jerked King's hand back to his rifle. With the maddening elusiveness of darkness it was impossible to tell whether the sound was farther away or closer than the convergence of the paths. King's rifle muzzle swung to cover the spot and his left hand reached desperately again to feel for the Masai's waist band in which the light was struck.

Normally the big fellow would have understood the first nudge. Had it been elephants or lions or crawling head hunters, he would have been standing with it ready to hand. But in the presence of ghosts the plain African of him rendered him witless. It was a tribute to his dogged loyalty to his master that he stood beside him at all, instead of with the Hottentot in a tree.

AS KING felt for the light his rifle muzzle perforce wavered. It touched something. Before his reaching hand could snap back to it a startled noise sounded. A great paw smashed against the gun and whirled it from his hand.

In the fractional flash of thought before action King experienced a rifleman's anguish at the clunk of its oiled mechanism into debris. In the next flash he ducked low from whatever might bo swinging higher up and dived for the sound of the gun.

A yell came from the Masai. "*We-weh! Auni, Bwana!* Help! It has me!"

That was the first time in all their association together that King had heard that proud fighting man call for help. He sprang from where he was, arms and legs wide to grapple whatever might be. He hoped only that he might not impale himself on the Masai spear, and, tailing that, he hoped he might find it so that he would have a weapon.

The impact of landing on a welter of writhing limbs knocked a grunt from him. His arms grappled partly with a something of immense power and partly with the smooth form of the Masai. A flash of comfort was to feel the man's great muscles alive and strong in defense.

King clawed at the shagginess that whirled him about like a puppet. He himself could have given even the great Masai a tussle. But this thing plunged as enormously as something prehistoric. A great paw at his back hugged his wounded side excruciatingly close. Momentarily he expected the crunch of great teeth or the disemboweling slash of claws. If only he could see something to avoid, to attack! The best he could do in the enveloping blackness was to pound at the bulk with his fists.

He smashed at it with all the strength that desperation gave him. Grunts came from the thing. Fending off with one hand, King was feeling for his hunting knife when his feet cart-wheeled from under him and he was down.

On the ground he fought instinctively as the primitive things of the jungle fight, on his back, arms high to protect his throat, feet drawn up to guard his stomach. Sounds of fight threshed over him.

A weight lurched down on his feet. As lions do, he kicked mightily with both together. He did not know whose the weight might be, but he heaved with all his loins and back and thighs. The weight was too great for the Masai's, but King could move it. It staggered back and the lumpy thud of its fall sounded.

For the moment free! Both of them!

"The flashlight, fool!" King yelled and he dived again to grope for his rifle.

The Masai's voice brought a surge of thankfulness—only because it showed that he lived. What the voice panted smashed the moment of joy.

"The light, *Bwana,* is lost."

And then hopefulness surged back. The heavy padding feet— retreating!

"The moonlit patch!" The Hottentot's voice screamed from above. "In three breaths the ghost will pass through it!"

The *pad, pad* went faster.

"There!" shrilled the Hottentot.

And at the same moment came King's shout as his fingers touched metal.

"*Awaie!*" the Hottentot wailed. "How fearful a thing to see! My eyes fear to look!"

King's rifle was snapping to his shoulder as he rolled. He saw the thing lurch into the moon patch. A monstrous form, pale in the filtered glow and vaguely outlined in the leaf pattern. A something that moved, that was all. But great arms were discernible writhing upwards, and the thing ran on its hind feet like a man.

King's finger froze on the trigger. He held his fire for just that hesitant second. And then the thing was gone. Only sounds told that it ever had been.

All in the space of a fleeting second. So fleeting that it was lost in the blackness again before the Masai's superstitious anguish broke and the Hottentot's monkey chittering was not up in the tree, but grovelling about King's feet.

King got up slowly. He breathed hugely, looking after the thing's passing. Then, "Let's get out of here," he said shortly, and gave no other word until they were well out of the jungle.

"*Eweh!*" The Masai shook himself. "*Jini wa 'Ngagi,* The father spirit of all the great apes. *Wah!* It shall go down to my children that I, an Elmoran of the Masai, clung to that ghost with all my might until *Bwana* should find means to slay it."

"Oh?" said King. "You were clinging to it, were you? No wonder. And what did you see, Apeling?"

Kaffa the Hottentot had his own theology. "It was Heitzi Eibib, who created all the trees and growing things and who sometimes walks amongst them on the ground to see how his work prospers."

"Both of which," King said dryly, "are amongst the reasons why white men continue to dominate Africa."

HE SAID no more until he came to Hawkes' bungalow and hammered on the door. Hawkes was as profuse with greeting and relief as his breeding would let him express.

"Awf'ly glad you're back, old man. I've been thinking I shouldn't have let you go. Did you get it?"

"First," King said, "some government hospitality. A cup of your ghastly coffee to settle my ragged nerves, and then I'll talk."

Not till he had grimaced over a cup of acrid pale brown liquid did he satisfy Hawkes' insistent questioning with one word.

"Tarzan."

"You mean, the monster is a—You don't mean to tell me it's a man?"

"A man, and nothing else," King said positively. "But a great brute of a man. And a white man! As naked as a raw tusk, and as batty as a loon. What you got to say to that, Copper, in your district where white men are few and you're supposed to know every one of them and everything that's going on?"

The surprise began to die out of Hawkes' face.

"A district as big as your Texas," he murmured. "But we do have a way of knowing what's going on, old fellow." He went to his desk and found a letter, a portentous thing with a crest on it, "If this chap is a man, he must be Mister Carlo Bentinck's gorilla man. But what he's doing, howling in the woods at night, I don't know, unless he escaped or something."

It was King's turn to stare. "What's Carlo Bentinck's gorilla man?"

"Mr. Carlo Bentinck," Hawkes' smile was very superior, "has a freak of some sort. He has offered a proposition of some sort to Sir Harry Jenks, and Sir Harry has asked me"—Hawkes' smile twisted wryly—"He has, er—ordered me to investigate Carlo before he considers doing business."

King snorted. "Huh, him? Just like a hang-bellied prince of industry to guard his pennies, looking up a man's record before making a deal, instead of just looking at his face and gambling on what he knows of men. And what right has a tourist like him to go handing out orders to the local police?"

Hawkes stiffened. "He's a very important person, old man. Got oodles of oof, you know. And the last birthday honors list made him Sir Harry."

King snorted again. "You chums sure have a knack of keeping the rest of the world guessing. Here's you with your whole system based on a hereditary aristocracy, and you take some lard by-products champion and think to add him to the high hat list by giving him a title. A crest on his letter head. Pah! What is it? A hog on a dinner plate?"

Hawkes was dutifully shocked. "Oh, I say, old chap. That's laying it on a bit thick, don't you think?"

"All right, all right," King grumbled. "Only I heard how he fired Tommy Ansell, as good a guide as you got in the land, for not agreeing with him fast enough. What's this deal that a freak manager has with your birthday aristocrat?"

"I don't really know. Sir Harry didn't condescend to tell me— just ordered me to investigate this Carlo fellow. Had to admit I could find out nothing on short notice, so he asked me to be present at the meeting and look him over."

"And," said King, "you'll take me along. Since I came damn near to shooting his new freak last night I'm interested enough to see your Sir High Hat take over the management and stick him a fat price for going out and bringing his pet back alive."

"Oh it's nothing like that," Hawkes said. "I mean, not a freak show. It's something or other about some medicinal product, as far as I could gather. Dashed mysterious and all. Matter of fact, old chap, I *would* like you to come along and give me your opinion."

CHAPTER II

THE JUJU'S SECRET

THE LITTLE hotel, as every patriotic one should, contained a "royal suite," and in it was Sir Harry Jenks. Sir Harry received Hawkes with a studied dignity and just a little more aloofness than his superior officer might have affected. At King's informal attire he raised bushy, graying eyebrows.

"My deputy, sir," Hawkes explained.

King's eyelids flickered and the side of his face towards Hawkes grinned.

"The Bentinck person," Sir Harry drawled, "is waiting some-where about the place with his prodigy. I'll 'ave—" He replaced the *h* with an effort—"I shall have him summoned."

King stiffened to interest. "*With* his critter, you say?"

Sir Harry's eyes stared at King over their well-fed pouches without reply.

A brisk footstep sounded in the hallway, overlaid by a pon-derous shuffling of dragged feet. A brisk knock, and an alert, sparely built man entered. But neither King nor Hawkes looked at him. Their eyes hung on the mountainous thing that sham-bled after him.

An immense man. By no means the freak that King had expected, no throwback to the anthropoid. His arms and legs under loose drill shirt and pants were in proportion to shoulders that almost filled the doorway. Just one great brute of a man. Only his eyes were dull under lowered lids and his heavy face was blankly without expression.

Sir Harry's only introduction was: "The local police. You will please repeat to them what you told me."

King examined the Bentinck man now. A wiry figure, swarthy and well bronzed, with a nervously intense manner. A man who had obviously been places and knew how to take care of himself. But his nervousness was in no way occasioned by the presence of the police. He smiled confidently at them with strong, even teeth and produced, first, a photograph.

"Observe, please, this picture, gentlemen."

It was a picture of a big boned man, tall and cadaverous; as tall as the huge fellow, a good six foot six. Only in his leanness he looked even taller.

"That was taken six years ago." Bentinck said. "Now look at Hermann here. Hermann," he commanded sharply. "Look this way."

The huge fellow lifted his head and turned lack-luster eyes on the police. Bentinck smiled on them and nodded his an-ticipation of their agreement.

"The same, is it not? No question about that, is there? Right. Now let me show you. Hermann. Attention! Show strength. Strong, understand? Show." He flexed his own arms to make his meaning clear.

The dull eyes looked slowly away and about the room. Then a long arm reached out with the vast deliberation of a giant sloth and picked up a heavy chair as easily as though it were a pillow.

"Not that!" Bentinck shouted.

But the slow brain impulses had been started. The great hands and shoulders, as slowly as the mind that actuated them, bunched to exert a twisting pressure. The chair cracked like tree limbs in a hurricane and came apart in those tremendous hands.

"Bad, Hermann!" Bentinck scolded. "Sit down! Very bad! I am now compelled to pay for that."

Hermann slowly subsided, a look of hurt incomprehension on his face. Bentinck's smile was triumphant.

"Now, gentlemen, you will be asking how that can happen in six short years, and I shall tell you. But first I shall ask you this: Both of you have observed monkeys, is it not—even the great apes, perhaps. Yes? You know then that a chimpanzee of fifty pounds is stronger than a grown man. You should not care to have to fight one. No. I ask you, then, why? I ask you, what is it that supplies to the apes a vitality and a muscular development so far in excess of human attainment?"

The strong white teeth flashed.

"I will tell you why, gentlemen—because of an element in their diet that civilized humanity lacks."

He let the thought sink in while he took another breath. "There can be no question in the face of patent fact. The cave man could hold his own with his anthropoid cousin. It is civilized man who has lost that vital element. And I, gentlemen, I have rediscovered it!" He flung his hand to point out Hermann. "The proof!" He leaned forward and his voice dropped to punctuated solemnity. "In six years!"

H E S T O O D back to survey his audience. His outflung hand swept the room. "And, gentlemen, I believe—I hope—that Sir Harry Jenks, with his wide experience of business, has the vision to see the commercial value of this vital element, properly exploited and placed upon the market. Not only the strength of the gorillas can be built up in man—but the vitality, the tireless energy that civilization has sapped from man, restored. Consider but for a moment the possibilities." He bowed towards Sir Harry. "To you, sir, I do not need to point them out. Just the discovery of this vital element, eh, in a great advertising campaign for a breakfast cereal?"

Sir Harry nodded. It was easy to see that sales points were revolving in his mind. King's face remained angularly wooden.

Hawkes was struggling with an obvious question. Bentinck forestalled it.

"You are going to ask me why, then, do I offer to share so valuable a discovery? I will tell you the truth. I told you that I had rediscovered this element. The truth is that Hermann has discovered it, and I—" He struck his chest—"I have rediscovered Hermann!"

"You ought to take better care of so valuable a critter," King said curtly. "I came damned near to shooting him a couple nights back."

Hermann's overhung brows jerked and his dull eyes lit in a quick sidewise flash; then he slumped again in dull apathy.

Bentinck's hand flew to his lips.

"You nearly shot my Hermann when he was woods running, loose by the full moon? My poor Hermann, who cannot take care of himself?"

Explanation poured from him in a shaken voice. "Six years ago, gentlemen, Hermann and I were partners, prospecting. We lost one another. At that time he was as you see him in the photograph. Then he was—" Bentinck tapped his own head— "the same as you and I. During that period, gentlemen—I do not yet know all the details, but Hermann has lived with the apes in the lost Kafu River country."

"Ha!" It burst from King. "In the country of the One-Eyed Juju."

Bentinck whirled on him. "You know that country?"

"Only the edges." King said. "Never went in, account of hostile natives."

"But then you understand perfectly." Bentinck's teeth flashed. "And you can substantiate my statement. To go in there requires, frankly, a strong party. When I found my poor Hermann again, gentlemen, he led me back to that country. But—" He shrugged. "As you might well know, I was driven out. We got away with barely our skins. But I have seen it, gentlemen." Bentinck's voice rose, "I have even tasted this element that builds such vitality— a leaf, not unlike tea or coffee. It is prolific. It is—" His hands fell to his sides; he swung to face Sir Harry, his voice quiet and appealing. "I do not have to tell you, sir, that such a medicament is worth money. You yourself are better able to judge of its commercial possibilities than am I. And there it lies. It requires, first investigation, then development." Bentinck flung wide his arms in surrender. "It needs the financing of a safari."

Sir Harry nodded in full understanding. He said: "I am inclined to go into the matter with you. Er—on a business basis, of course. I shall give you my answer tomorrow. You may go now. And take your—" He pointed a thick finger at the indescribable Hermann, turned to Hawkes. "And you will also give me your opinions tomorrow. That is all."

"WELL?" HAWKES demanded. "What d'you make of it all? Is there any such bally stuff?"

King shrugged. "I'd bet ten to one against it. But don't ask me to say what fantastic thing can be in Africa and what can't."

"What do you make of the blighter, then?"

King turned the question back. "You're the sleuth. What do you?"

"Well, the fellow is a foreigner of some sort, in spite of his

*A great paw smashed against the gun
and whirled it from his hand.*

good English, and I don't trust any of those chappies until I know something more about 'em."

"Old Johnny Bull." King twisted a sour face over the strong tea. "Fellow's a foreigner, not of the good old stock. Hang him."

"Well then, my dear fellow, if you judge people only by their face, what do you think?"

"He's not a fool. And he's got his guts. And he's a good actor and a showman. All of which, if he's cooking snake meat, could mean grief for the guests."

"Humph! Sort of cheering news for the police, what?"

"I'll tell you something less cheering. Did you notice Tarzan wake up when I said I nearly shot him? He understood that fast enough."

"By jove! No! What d'you think that might mean?"

"Nothing—yet. But if it was a publicity stunt to catch our Harry's attention, and if our Hermie should happen to be a good actor too; then that lad with that kind of a face and those gorilla-food muscles, could mean howling murder in some of its messier forms. And I'll tell you something else. Your Sir High-opera-hat Harry is sold up to his neck to go in on this proposition, and his asking your opinion is only so he can blame all the mishaps on the office boy."

Hawkes sat sucking in the ends of his military moustache. "I'm afraid so, old man. And the deuce of it is we can't afford to let him run into danger; he's a frightfully important personage."

"You can't stop those big money boys," King said callously. "Not when they smell a promotion racket with a chance for big sucker dough. I'll bet you right now that our friend Harry is fixing to go on this expedition."

Hawkes shook his head. "Good Lord! We can't afford to let him get hurt." He sat drumming the fingers of his unwounded arm on his chair. "Dash it all. If I wasn't out of commission I'd go along myself. But—"

"No you don't," King shouted. "You don't get me to go pulling any hot chestnuts out of any African fire for your development of colonial industries."

Hawkes, in his staunch conception of service to Empire, could see not a thing preposterous in such an idea. "But damn it all, my dear fellow, don't you see if he gets into that Kafu country he might get himself—" Hawkes wouldn't put the appalling thought into words.

"Sure he will," King said complacently. "Fires a good man like Tommy Ansell, who might have kept him out of trouble.

So he'll go with these con artists. And if they know enough to show him a juju sign of monkey skull and snake skin that says, 'Hurry up and stay outa here,' he'll pooh-pooh it and barge on through. Nobody can keep him out; he barges right into prime ministers' offices. So he'll get a spear shoved through his middle, and little loss to the world. I know a lot of honest spear shovers I like better'n him."

Hawkes pointed his finger at King and crooked the thumb beneath it like a gun. "Bango, old chap. You've said it yourself. That's exactly what would happen."

"And so what? I've seen it happen to better men in Africa."

"So—" Hawkes punctuated his points, throwing down his pointing finger as though shooting directly between King's eyes—"we'd have to send in troops. I tell you he rates jolly near as important as visiting royalty. If they should do him in, it would mean a punitive expedition. You've seen 'em, haven't you?"

"You bet I have." King's cheerful complacency vanished in indignation. "A thousand dumb blacks mowed down with machine-guns, because some hang-bellied prince of finance is close enough to a tin god to rate his profits like a national religion. Damn, I've done my share, but I've done it alone; no blasted army to come mopping up after my hard luck."

"And," Hawkes added, "after the army, a ten-year hang-over of hate before a man like you can trade that district again."

King sat scowling over the veranda rail.

"And," Hawkes put in gently, "if this chappie comes to grief while he's in my hands, may career is shot. I may as well fold up and go home."

King transferred his scowl to Hawkes. Hawkes' eyes held his.

"I'll give you," said Hawkes, "two native constables as escort, and Sir Harry already knows you as my deputy."

"Two!" King's derision flared. "Two whole constables to nursemaid a tin godling through a thousand square miles of hostile territory! What d'you think I am—a Texas Ranger?"

"I don't know your Texas Rangers." Hawkes said. "But our South African Constabulary have handled as big a situation."

King's scowl worked all around his face. "They have, huh?" His jaw muscles chewed on that. "But they had official authority."

"You'll have authority. My deputy. Emergency situation and all that. Needs a white man leader."

KING'S JAW muscles bunched. Then it came from him vindictively. "Listen, Copper. If I'm crazy enough to do this for you, if I ever drag that slob out alive, I'll expect absolution in advance for a list of crimes against your silly government it'll take me ten years to catch up with." He nodded a certain satisfaction at the prospect. "And I won't do it for your blasted colonial prestige either, nor for your precious plutocrat. I'll do it so a thousand naked spearmen won't get cut in half by machine-guns. And for just one other reason."

Hawks suspected an admission of friendly sentiment and he shrank Britishly from it with a face already reddening. "Oh, I say, my dear chap. Don't say you would do it on my account. What I mean, a fellow doesn't talk about—"

"Yeah, on your account," King said grimly. "And for nothing else. Because this district needs a copper just like you—a stiff-necked, duty-ridden dumb one that I can slip things over on easy."

Hawkes reached out the hand that was not strapped to his side. "I'll give you the same two native constables that you rescued from that slave gang. They'd die for you."

"And that's a truth,' King growled. "They likely enough will—"

"And I'll give you this." Hawkes pulled open a drawer and shook moth balls from a uniform jacket. "It'll be a bit tight over your shoulders, but—proof of your authority." With a tinge of pride he added, "Something that's known all over Africa."

King only laughed sourly "White man juju, huh? Maybe I'll

*"They have
him, Bwana!"*

hang it on a pole for the black boys to come and pray to. Crazy business. Me on your side the fence. Hah!"

"AN ESCORT, eh?" Sir Harry raised his bushy brows at Hawkes. "Is that necessary?"

"Unsettled country, sir." Hawkes said. "And since you insist on going, we thought—"

Sir Harry cleared his throat and his sharp eyes made it quite clear that what Hawkes thought didn't matter. "Under command of your deputy fellow, eh? I suppose he'll take his orders from me."

Hawkes showed his national diplomacy. "Best man in the country, sir. I really ought to take charge myself, but—" He indicated his bandaged shoulder.

"Oh, of course, Captain." Sir Harry inclined his somewhat mottled face in perfect understanding. "Well, I suppose the man and I will get along all right." He said that in the certain tone of an executive with whom everybody in his entourage had always very carefully got along.

At about the same time Mister Carlo Bentinck was saying just about the same thing to King.

"An escort? So the police think it is advisable, yes?"

"That's the orders," King said cryptically. "His Nibs is an important pillar of the home aristocracy."

There was something about it that didn't hit quite the proper angle of respect.

"Regular force?" Bentinck asked shrewdly.

"Nope. Special deputy. Emergency case. His Nibs pays the extra grub wide and handsome."

"Ah!" Bentinck appraised the don't-give-a-damn grin on King's face, his distinctly "informal" uniform of khaki shooting coat and military puttees. "Ah! I think we shall get along."

"I get along with anybody who knows more'n I do," King said. "And with anybody who knows less and admits it. So I'm checking up on your safari equipment."

"Oh, certainly." Bentinck was confident about that.

"You bought a Jeffries .475 for him, I know. At a fancy price. It'll kick him endways if he ever shoots it off, but that's okay by me. And you billed him for two others, new, though they're seconds left over from the Pajet expedition."

Bentinck watched King as warily as a wolf. "You know about that?"

"We have a way," King said loftily, "of knowing what's going on." He was getting a ribald enjoyment out of his unwonted association with the Law. "One rifle is an extra, I suppose, 'cause you've hired no other gunners and Hermie doesn't shoot."

The Hermann creature was sitting, enormously inert, on the tailboard of a truck, admiring with the fondness of a butcher a tool that he fondled in his lap, a shiny new broad axe of the largest size that came.

"No," Bentinck admitted. "Hermann does not shoot."

"And looks like he don't need to," King said dryly. "And you bought two trucks, seconds, from Tommy Ansell at the top price too. That's not my worry. What you stick a financial wizard who knows too much to take advice is none of my business."

Bentinck nodded appreciation of so much understanding. "I am *sure* we shall get along."

"There's a chance of that too," King said. "But lemme advise you. If you want to get along with our fat friend you'd better pick a good cook and some snappy camp boys. Let's look at your grub list. When I'm on my own I travel lean. But here's the first time in my life the aristocracy feeds me."

CHAPTER III

ROAD TO DARKNESS

SAFARI, THAT so grandiloquent term insisted upon by rich sports and cynically acquiesced to by guides, is no longer a picturesque affair of a hundred black porters carrying little bundles on their heads, winding like mottled snakes over the vast African plains. It is a practical de luxe affair of trucks with strengthened springs that can leave the roads and lurch away over ant hills and roots as sturdily almost as a caterpillar tractor.

White men jounce on the front seats. African camp boys cling precariously wherever piled tents and food crates permit.

The old hazard of water holes has been eliminated by machinery that can carry water by the hogshead. The only "roughing it" left comes of having to sleep in tents where doors cannot be locked against prowling carnivora.

Yet Sir Harry found room for complaint. He complained because it was not fitting that the Masai and Hottentot, with the efficiency of long practice, had King's personal tent pitched and old kerosene can of water heated, and King was lounging his length on a cot, bath and luxuriating with a pipe, while Sir Harry's own canvas still billowed in the evening wind under the astoundingly inept hands of tourist camp boys.

Fuming, he called to King from where he stood under a mimosa tree. Leisurely King got off his cot and obliged, his pipe still in the corner of his mouth.

"I say, my man," Sir Harry snapped. "Your fellows seem to have more experience in all this."

King smiled benignly. "They're good. About the best in Africa. Though Ansell has some pretty near as good."

"Well, damn it, why don't they help?" he demanded.

King shook his head. "They're just escort. They and the two constables and me, we're just along to see that nobody bops you on the head."

Sir Harry stared at King, while the mottled grayness of his cheeks reddened with the fury of a man whose mere suggestions had always constituted an order. And then—give him credit— he called for no outside help.

"Damn your impudence, you bounder!" he shouted and he aimed a furious swipe at King's head.

Without removing his pipe, King slipped his head under the savage swing, stepped in and pinioned Sir Harry's arms above both elbows. He grinned at him.

"Takes practice," he said. "You don't get it in a director's office." He gripped the elbows with his thumbs excruciatingly in the soft hollows until Sir Harry's futile struggles ceased. Then he let go and stepped back.

Even through his rage Sir Harry recognized the uselessness of repetition. It had never in his life occurred to him that anything so blasphemous as retaliation could happen to him. He swallowed many times before his splutter came through, strangling in his throat.

"I'll have you dismissed from the force for this, you ruffian."

King remained astonishingly cheerful in the face of the tirade.

"True to form," he said. "Only that's one you just can't do."

Sir Harry didn't understand the irony of that situation. He fumed.

"I'll turn back immediately and obtain more efficient servants."

King nodded. "Yeah, you could do that. Only I don't know whether your safari conductor would want to now, four days out an' all."

The thought was a sobering shock to Sir Harry. He swung startled eyes to Bentinck, half expecting to see him already hastening to his help.

Bentinck was bending over some camp gear, studiously avoiding any interference.

That the loyalty of his hirelings could ever be in doubt was another horrid experience to Sir Harry. The first moment of it awed him as though it were a phenomenon reversing all the forces of Nature.

"Would the fellow dare to—would 'e 'ave the bloody himpudence to mutiny?" Sir Harry's carefully acquired aitches reverted, in his agitation, to their original chaos.

"I wouldn't know," King said gravely. "You didn't consult the police when you fixed up your safari arrangements with him."

The police! Law and Order! The things that Sir Harry had almost forgotten in his mighty career as being the forces that backed up his authority, away back in his sheltered civilization. He whirled back on King with a Briton's stout reliance on service.

"You scoundrel. You're supposed to represent the Law."

"Sure do," King grinned at him. "Got my juju right in my blanket roll there. You just appeal to the Law that you want to go home and I'll take you back if I have to shoot up the camp. That's all I'm here for, to bring you back alive; and nobody'd be more pleased than me, mister, that I'd be through with the chore that easy. Only—"

"Only what?" Sir Harry's business instinct remained wary of unforseen contingencies.

"Only there would go all your chances of your monkey food. The Law can't order Hermie to guide you."

Sir Harry digested that thought in sulky silence. Then the driving force of his life, business profits, took its normal ascendancy.

"I shall go on," he said doggedly.

"Okay by me," said King. "I'm only escort."

H E   W E N T back to his own tent and did a thing most undignified for the majesty of the law. He hunkered down beside the little fire with his men. The Masai took a horn container from the lobe of his ear and out of it tapped a pinch of snuff upon his great spear blade and reached it across the fire. King took a few grains and went through the motion of sniffing. It was a sign that this was an informal fireside chat, off the record.

"If *Bwana* had but called," the Masai growled, "with a throwing spear I would from here have nailed that disrespectful one to the tree."

"And so would have caused much trouble, Barounggo, old blood-letter," King said. "Here is wit needed. Kaffa, what do you make of this trek after four days? Particularly of your Heitzi Eibib with his great axe?"

The two constables, who had not been through that fear, guffawed their superiority. The Hottentot scuffled his abashment and muttered: "So bellow the cattle, safe under their herd guard. As to that first born of'Ngagi the great Ape Father, my observation tells me this: All this trail is new to him. He knows nothing of it. He leads us nowhere. But his keeper knows."

"Ah!" said King. "So I have thought. But that is perhaps because that great one's wit is no greater than his brother ape."

"Nay, *Bwana*. A little, though not much greater, than an ape's." The little imp scuttled around to the other side of the fire. "For he, too, can use speech."

"Ha! That's what I've been trying to find out. How do you know that?"

"In the night, *Bwana*, I have lain close beside their tent flap, and I have heard him talk softly with his keeper as men talk who have secrets, only in a language that I do not know."

King stared, narrow-eyed, into the fire, "What secret evil those two hatch we must find out. Yet have a care, Apeling. That keeper is no greenhorn. Awake, he might have heard you."

The Hottentot chittered the triumph of a monkey that has escaped the penalty of its inveterate inquisitiveness. "It is the other one who has the ears of an animal. Last night that ox suddenly burst forth and nearly set his great foot on me. But when did the buffalo ever catch the *ngedere* monkey that sees by night? From under his very hooves I fled."

"Oho! So that was that noise. Watch it, Little Wise One, watch it. That axe blade would span your belly in one stroke."

The Hottentot remained careless. "So long as it is not a ghost, *Bwana*, my belly does not turn to water and loosen my limbs."

"Watch it none the less, Apeling, and the three of you besides. It is up to the *policea* chief Hawkes' honor that we bring this stubborn man of much money and no knowledge back alive."

WHILE CAMP boys frittered away the usual two hours or so over getting gear stowed, King talked with Bentinck, who ought to have had it stowed an hour ago.

"W'hereabouts d'you aim to hit this Kafu jungle? There's quite a belt of it."

"Wherever Hermann leads to, of course," Bentinck said.

"Looked to me like he wasn't leading any place," King said bluntly. "Seemed like all this territory was new to him."

Bentinck studied King from out the corner of one eye. He said:

"My poor Hermann. No, he does not with deliberation lead. He retraces rather his path by an unreasoning instinct almost of an animal."

"I've seen animals get lost when they're being chased out of a district."

Bentinck's white teeth flashed. "In this case it would not matter so much, for we must at the last come to a Kafu tributary on the south bank called the Inridi. It is not on the map."

"Oho! You got quite a ways into the juju country before they chased you out. Why shove so far into trouble? Is your valuable stuff found only there?"

"Yes." Bentinck's teeth were avid. "It is found only there."

"Then if you know the place, why drag Hermie along?"

That should have been a poser. But Bentinck smiled up at King and King knew that it was a polite refusal to disclose secrets.

"My friend, by the time I get to that Kafu tributary I might have forgotten all about that valuable leaf—I mean, the appearance and the taste of it."

King looked at the man and smiled too, though through thin lips.

"What you mean is it's none of my business."

Bentinck shrugged.

"Why could it not mean, my friend, that you said you could get along with anybody who knew more than you; and so I maintain myself just a little bit ahead." His laugh was almost a challenge.

But not to anything so absurd as physical combat. King knew that. And for the present he preferred to let things rest.

THE HOTTENTOT'S sleuthing was not much more

successful, though much more troublesome. It was his ineradicable urge to pit the keenness of his wit against massive brawn that impelled him to the perilous business of trying to draw out Hermann.

He busied himself in company with the camp boys. His reasoning was that if Hermann knew any of the African dialects, one might begin to get a line on Hermann. His technique was crude but effectively simple. With one wary eye on Hermann he made derogatory remarks about him in Swahili. He used the commonest words that every white man learns within his first month, because he must call them at blundering servants. *Mkombokombu,* great lout, and *mpumbafu,* half-wit—with an acrid tongue he applied the terms to Hermann, who sat with the lowering vacancy of a none too great intellect on his countenance, nursing the great broad-axe.

Hermann's face remained blank to Swahili. But the camp boys laughed hugely at the crude wit. The Hottentot tried in Arabic, in Masai, in Zulu. He drew upon wherever his wanderings with his master had taken him and whatever vituperation he had added to his arsenal of acid speech that did him duty in place of other men's weapons.

Slow-witted Hermann was, but not so foolish as to remain heedless to the covert looks of the camp boys as they guffawed and not so dull as not to know that he was being laughed at, nor yet so without reason as not to guess that this obtrusive little imp might well be the eavesdropper of two nights ago.

Yet close enough to all three was Hermann to be ever suspicious of ridicule and accordingly ungovernable in animal rage.

The first that King knew was Kaffa's shrill screech of fear, and as he whirled in instant defense to the call, there was the Hottentot racing over the plain, and after him Hermann, with his great axe.

Like a frantic baboon the Hottentot ran, hopping from one high grass tussock to the next, dodging round tall ant hills, his wisp of blanket trailing in the wind, shrieking in his extremity.

Hermann like a vengeful buffalo lunged behind him, making enormous swipes with his axe.

King's rifle was at his back, hung from his left shoulder by its sling. He jerked his shoulder with an expert movement and the rifle made a neat, close half circle around the shoulder and smacked into his left hand; his right in the same smooth movement snatched the bolt out and back. He stood so, watchful, set like a tempered spring to act.

Bentinck, standing beside him, was almost as fast. His right hand slid under his shirt and he held it so, watching not the impending murder on the plain, but King's every move.

King's eyes remained grimly on the runners, his rifle half raised, like a ready skeet shooter. But out of the corner of his mouth he said to Bentinck:

"Just try drawing it, feller, and see if, among all the other things, you know more about guns than I do."

Bentinck's eyes flicked from King's granite profile to his taut shoulders, to his hands, fully occupied with his rifle, too close to swing the muzzle round. He tried it.

King's eyes never left the racing men, nor his rifle muzzle their direction. But he snatched a second to slam the butt back under his right arm. It thudded into Bentinck's chest and knocked him rolling. King couldn't see the full effect of it; but for all the possibility that the man might still be deadly, he dared not take his eyes off the death behind his racing Hottentot.

Protection to his servants was a creed that won for King a loyalty that many another Africander wondered at and envied; and King gambled now on the reciprocal service that he expected. His voice said to Bentinck, out of his sight:

"Before you try anything else, better look around and see if my Masai isn't in on the play somewhere."

The sheer cool confidence of it impelled Bentinck to do just as he was advised. He looked, and he lay very still.

A SCANT twenty feet from him the Masai poised, a splendid naked statue of a javelin thrower in black marble. Legs wide, torso inclined, arm flung back, his spear on a level with his ear. The morning sun threw silky high lights from his great muscles and glinted silvery from the long blade.

The whole camp remained frozen in action as though a cog in a motion picture projector had jammed; the principal actors tense on the point of a single tooth, ready to go as soon as the gears might mesh, the supers staring white-eyed. Motionless, everybody.

The only objects that moved were the Hottentot and his pursuer, dwindling into the distance. And it was distance that released the action, distance and stamina. The little Hottentot drew away from the lumbering Goliath. Goliath slowed down, came to a stop. The Hottentot pranced on a tall ant hill and screeched vituperation at him.

King lowered his rifle and his smile broke tightly round his mouth.

"*Whau!*" The Masai intoned his deep exclamation that signified satisfaction over any happening, whether a good meal or a killing, and he came to life.

Bentinck got up slowly. He said to King, "I admit it—you know more about guns than I do."

"Meaning you want to get along?"

Bentinck nodded. "You and I, if we could but once come to an understanding, could make a profit out of this. No hard feelings, yes?"

"Nary one—yet," said King. "Not over a thing like this. It's just Africa."

"Then tell me." Bentinck asked. "So that I may understand. Would you have shot Hermann?"

There was not a flicker of evasion on King's face.

"Sure thing," he said. "My Hottentot looks like a monkey but he's a whole little heap of man; and your Hermie looks like a man but—" He looked at Bentinck without any hint of a smile. "You said yourself he was pretty close to an animal."

Bentinck stared at him, perplexed. "You are very difficult to understand, my friend,"

King grinned cheerfully at his perplexity. "Stick with your game, guy, and you may find out sometime." He turned from him and went to the Masai.

"That was well and readily done, old warrior," he said. "There will be a gift of a cow for your father's *kraal*. And our Apeling will thank you for saving him from his ghost, from whom he hoped to make his honor clean by entrapping it into speech."

"*Whau!*" the Masai said. "It was a little thing, *Bwana*, to have open eyes in the daylight and to be ready. As for that great ghost—" He stopped to scratch thoughtfully at the side of his neck with his yard of spear blade—"I, too, have an honor to make clean with him."

Bentinck came up. He said: "One more thing I admit. You have more experience than I in picking a way through the easiest ground. Do you, then, lead with your truck and Sir Jenks. I will tell you which way to go."

"You won't have to," King said. "I know the best way to your Inridi tributary of the Kafu."

Sir Harry stood looking on at these doings, for the first time in his life a silent bystander. His mottled shadings stood out against the whiteness of his cheeks likes daubs of gray paint. The closeness of sudden death and the casualness of it left him, for the first time too, with no orders to give. But—grant him always his meager credit—he did not say that he wanted to go home.

KING ACCORDINGLY drove the lead truck, picking out ground by guess and by that observation of shrubbery growths a mile ahead that makes a sixth sense for the traveler of the veldt, until out of the wilderness there appeared a trail.

King swung into it and headed north. A mile behind him Bentinck's truck hooted and tooted frantic signals until King stopped. Bentinck was red-eyed with angry suspicion. Beside him Hermann sat, brows drawn heavy over his little eyes in a scowl that was a murderous threat.

King grinned at the obvious betrayal of intelligence.

"Looks like Hermie's animal instinct feels we're headed wrong."

Hermann's insensate rage very nearly overcame his acting. His mouth opened to blaze forth words. But Bentinck clapped his hand over the big man's mouth.

"What the hell game are you playing here?" he snarled. "The Kafu jungle is due west and you know it."

"Sure," King agreed. "A hundred miles of it. We'd have to leave the trucks and crawl afoot. But you don't want just jungle. Your funny tea leaves happen in just one spot, and getting there is something else I know better'n you. Here's a government road; it'll cross the Kafu at a ford. I'll turn east along the north bank where the map shows no jungle and I'll ferry you across at the Inridi in a canoe, slam into your juju country."

Bentinck said, "You can't. The natives are hostile; they keep their canoes hidden, sunk with rocks. That is one thing I know if you do not. I have been there."

"And I never have," King said. "But somebody will loan me a canoe." He grinned. "'Cause I'll get me a letter of introduction." He grinned wider, pointed his thumb to Sir Harry beside him. "But this isn't my safari; I'm not running it into any juju sacrifices to make a business profit. I'm only escort to see that the boss here gets out of it alive. Ask him what way he wants to go."

Sir Harry rose to his own life-long habit of decision. He said to King: "You are the most insolent man I have ever met. But I believe you can do what you say."

King flipped his hand in a derisive salute to Bentinck and meshed his gears.

Sir Harry sat in a stiff silence, too lofty to inquire what might be this extravagant mystery of so civilized a thing as a letter of introduction in the savage back land of Africa. But Kaffa, crouching behind on the angle of a chop box, chattered his eager intuition.

"*Bwana* goes to visit the witch doctor of the Kafu ford?"

King nodded into the heat haze ahead of him. "If there is one there, as I have heard."

"I too have so heard. A little one. Not like our Great One of Elgon. But to a friend of the Great One this one will disclose the hidden things."

"And hidden things are here that need disclosing. Those two are playing some monkey business about this juju country that doesn't mean any good to anybody else but themselves." He drove on, and the farther he went the harder the lines of his frown.

CHAPTER IV

THE WIZARD OF KAFU FORD

THE WIZARD of the Kafu ford lived on a hill; the transparent reason for which was that he might observe all comers and prepare his hocus-pocus for their bewilderment.

King took the Hottentot with him. They marched without subterfuge to the sign that said, "No admittance except on business." It said so by means of seven snake skins and an antelope skull attached to a tree with the horns pointed toward the oncomer's breast.

King knew enough of witch doctor etiquette not to push through. He sent the Hottentot ahead.

"Give him this blanket and the tobacco," he directed. "And pay him what compliments your wit may devise—and show him the carving that the Great One put on my pipe."

He sat down to wait while the Hottentot commenced the tedious business of crawling forward on all fours, beating his head on the ground and shouting the bonga ritual of praise.

Normally a witch doctor's dignity demands that his visitors be kept waiting over a period of time graded very carefully according to their rank, which is judged by the number of their followers. A man arriving with one scrawny Hottentot rated about two days of delay. But within five minutes the wizard appeared at the door of his hut. He made no hocus-pocus. He shouted as man to human man words that he had never spoken before.

"*Karib, Mzungu.* Be welcome, white man."

The witch doctor was not togged out in his professional paraphernalia of bones and dried reptiles and charms. He appeared as an ordinary human with keenly intelligent eyes in a shrewd old face.

With his own hands he set a three-legged stool for his guest in the shade of his hut and squatted simply beside it.

"My women will bring mealie beer," he said. "Honor has fallen upon me that the Great One of Elgon knows even my name."

King wondered just what fantastic inventions the Hottentot had woven into his complimentary message.

"To a friend of that Great One's," the wizard said naively, "since he sends me so good a blanket by the hand of his friend, I will tell the truth."

"A truth is what I need," King said. "About that juju country of the Inridi mouth."

"Ow!" said the wizard. "Mzungu would visit the country of the One-Eyed Juju?"

"A fool," said King, "led by a knave goes there. I go as guardian to the fool."

"*Wo-we!* That will be a difficult guarding. For the people of the juju have a feud against white men."

"So I have heard. Since a year ago, before which they were not unfriendly. Why then a feud?"

"Because a white man stole the juju. It was said that he was a doctor of white men's knowledge and he wanted to display it in a house where white men keep many strange things for their students to look at."

King muttered his disgust to himself. Same old story. Scientists, missionaries, what not, good Christians all, think because it's a naked savage's god it's something to swipe and stick in a museum. And then they yell for soldiers when the savage retaliates and sticks a white man's head on a bamboo juju pole.

The wizard understood none of it, but his trade was to read men's thoughts. He said: "Yes, the people of the juju were very angry; because it was a very good juju made of a black stone and it could talk."

King raised an eyebrow at that.

"Or at least," the wizard chuckled, "its head priest could talk from his stomach."

"Have there been killings yet?" King asked. "I mean, white men?"

But that was one thing no black man would tell a white man. The wizard said, "I do not know." And King knew perfectly well what he meant. He said:

"Tell me then another thing. Is there a leaf in that country that the great apes eat to make them strong?"

The wizard laughed. "It is a tale told by mothers to their children to make them eat foods that are tasteless. 'Look,' they say, 'the medicine is in the food and you will grow strong.' And the children, being inexperienced, do not know that it is the talent of women to gain their ends through lies. But foolish men believe the tale and come looking for that medicine. Yet, if there were such a medicine, I would surely have it and I would be greater than the Great One of Elgon."

"My fool believes the tale and comes looking, hoping to be greater than the great ones of his land."

The wizard spoke another truth out of his observation of men. "What a fool believes, he believes with all of a fool's stubbornness, and if there be a profit in the belief, even wise men become fools. Yet a knave cannot be a fool. What does the knave come looking for that is worth the risk of that juju country?"

"That is the truth that I hoped to find here," King growled.

"*Aie, Mzungu!* To read the evil in the mind of a man I have never seen is beyond my poor magic. The Great One of Elgon, perhaps. Not I. Ask easier things of me."

King stood up and shook himself, not entirely disappointed. "You have at least given me some information out of which truth may yet emerge. For the rest, since the knave has persuaded the fool there will be a profit, I'm afraid no talk of mine will stop us from going ahead and needing a canoe."

"I will send my silent voice out to those who can hear," the witch doctor said. "There will be a canoe. *Kua heri,* friend of the Great One of Elgon. My word is, go with care. My better word would be, slay the knave quickly before knavery brings death. But I know that white men have little wisdom in such a matter."

"Yeah," King said. "White man rules sure are a handicap when the other fellow hasn't any. *Kua heri,* Wizard. Send a good voice out for me."

THERE WAS a canoe. Whatever the wizard's methods of bush telegraph, the voice traveled faster than the trucks. Native villages en route remained peaceable; they even offered fowls and eggs for sale. King grinned at Bentinck's surly surprise.

"Something you ought to cultivate, my friend—a good reputation to leave behind you."

And when the safari arrived at the spot opposite to the Inridi River's inflow, there floated a big dugout with two natives in it. They said:

"A word came that white men would pay a just price for a boat. The price is five sticks of tobacco."

King stood with his feet planted wide and his thumbs in his belt, facing Sir Harry. He said, "Well, here's the last call. Across a hundred yards of river is whatever you're going to get, and I'll

"So is my word good."

tell you this: it won't be monkey food and it will be grief. Take
it or leave it. My advice is to leave it."

Bentinck cut in angrily to forestall Sir Harry. "You know a
lot suddenly, my too clever friend, do you not?"

"Yep, a whole lot," King said steadily. "But not quite everything—yet."

Sir Harry had been learning that King was not a man of false
alarms or loose statement. He said, "I am inclined to listen to
your judgment, if—"

Bentinck's darting eyes had already showed him that the
Masai was fifty yards away, superintending the unloading of
his master's baggage. The four white men stood along with just
the two canoe men gawping at Hermann and his giant axe. In
a frenzy of anxiety to forestall damning disclosures Bentinck
flung the ultimate taunt, and his hand was ready under his shirt.

"So our bold escort is suddenly now afraid, now that we are
on the brink of success."

King had lived his years through desperate situations by
never doing the expected. He disappointed Bentinck by grinning coolly.

"Sure I'm afraid," he admitted, "Did you ever see a juju sac-rifice?"

That was a turn of talk nearly as bad as disclosures. Bentinck appealed to the urge that had persuaded Sir Harry in the first instance.

"Do no let him fool you, sir. He is a man who draws just his day's pay whether he comes or goes. There is no profit in this for him. But for us, we are now here—we have a strong party. We—"

Sir Harry held up an authoritative hand. "Do not interrupt me again, either of you." He turned to King. "I was about to say I would be inclined to consider your objection if you would tell me where you obtained your information."

"The witch doctor two days back there told me."

Sir Harry first stared, and then smiled his disdain. "My good man! Really! The advice of a savage charlatan is hardly a suf-ficient reason to abandon a profitable business venture. We shall of course go on."

King shrugged. "Okay, mister. This isn't my safari. I'm only—" But he didn't finish that; he had said it often enough.

A DOZEN trips of the canoe ferried men and necessary baggage. Camp boys grumbled at having to divide the gear into small head packs and become porters. A weed-grown path, long disused, twisted from the sand spit into the jungle, following the general trend of the Inridi bank.

Kaffa loitered close to King and scratched aimless patterns on the sand with his toe. Only all the patterns aimed in the same direction—toward the jungle fringe across the river.

"Yes. I've seen 'em," King whispered. He moved away a short distance to where he could talk without the camp boys hearing and stampeding like bleating sheep. "How many, do you think?"

"Half a hundred, *Bwana,* and with spears."

"Huh. They don't waste time. Keep watch, Apeling, and tell Barounggo."

The two canoe men must have seen them too: they decided they wanted no connection with this white man party. With ape cunning they said no word, but slanted their canoe down the river; once on the other side, they brought no more baggage, but ducked around a bend and were gone.

For the first time on that safari King began to give orders. "Come along, you boys. Move your limbs there. Lift 'em; they aren't lead."

He herded them into the jungle path and then without question took the lead.

"Better set your gorilla to tail 'em and see there's no desertions," he told Bentinck.

Within a bare quarter mile the path, as could be expected, opened into a wide clearing. Dilapidated huts leaned drunkenly in its center. Deserted yam patches were overgrown with the yellow flowers of the mzabibu vine.

King took complete charge. "We camp right here,"

Bentinck said nothing. But Sir Harry resented the sudden assumption of authority.

"Why suddenly here?"

King was keyed up to alertness, in no mood to argue. He gave only acid reasons.

"Because I'm nobody's hired man. Because I've got a job with Captain Hawkes to get you out of here alive. Because we're here where your safari conductor said he had to come. So go ahead and ask him to show you his tea leaves. I'm going to be busy."

He plunged in amongst the camp boys, drove them to the clearing center, set them to clearing rubbish out of the most suitable huts, called Barrounggo to direct others in dismantling the outlying ones and piling the wreckage to make a stockade.

Whatever was Sir Harry's conference with Bentinck, he remained sufficiently dissatisfied to prefer King's advice. He came, almost friendly, at all events not condescending.

"Do you think there's danger?"

King remained grimly uncompromising. "There can always be danger in Africa. We came prepared for it, didn't we? We're strong enough—I think—to look after ourselves if we don't pull any fool boners."

"You think this is a good place?"

"The best. This is a ghost village."

"What is a ghost village? Why is it safe?"

"I never said it was safe. It's just the best we've got. Epidemic, catastrophe, something or other convinced the natives it was haunted by evil spirits. So they pulled out. Africa is full of ghost villages. Good thing about 'em is, nobody will come jumping us at night."

"They might by day?"

Sir Harry, King noted, was not cringing with nervous fear; he was asking sensible questions.

King shrugged. "They might. We'll have to make no mistakes."

"Well," Sir Harry said. "I'm not altogether a bad shot."

King fired a quickly commanding finger at him. "We don't want any fuss here if we can help it. Start shooting and that could be the boner that'd get us cleaned up. When I'm alone my hard luck is my own, but with you on my hands my hard luck would kick back on Hawkes. I don't know just what would happen to him; but I know damn well your army would come hopping down on these dumb savages with air bombs."

Sir Harry looked at King, puzzled.

"You are a very strange man," he said.

"Not strange." King's eyes were hot. "Just a plain guy of plain folks stock, and I never got so high, mister, that I could look down on the rest of 'em, whether white or black or yellow. These naked black boys have done nothing to us yet, and we—or some white man—has done plenty to them. White men have gone fighting crusades for no bigger a principle."

Perhaps back in his sumptuous offices in London, King's homely philosophy would have slid off the hard veneer of Sir

Harry's back; but here in the jungle clearing, with death waiting possibly just beyond the tree fringe, he was many flights closer to earth. He stared at the hard angularity of King's face, and walked slowly away, his eyes thoughtful.

AND THEN there was dusk falling as though it had been poured out of a tar barrel, the moon too late just now to break the solid shadows.

King made all the disposals of camp, set watchmen over little fires, told off his Masai and Hottentot to watch the watchmen, and showed the seriousness of it all by announcing that he would sit up and keep an eye on all of it.

In the camp's quietness Bentinck sat down beside King on a great flat topped log that had once been a dining table and siesta couch for its owners. He said:

"So we have arrived, yes. I do not yet understand you, but I am convinced that you and I should get along."

King grunted noncommittally.

"You and I are men much alike. We make our living by what we know of Africa and by what we dare."

"Hmh!"

"With what I know we could make a nice quick profit here."

King yawned, but his eyes narrowed. "Thought you'd picked Hermie for your strong-arm guy."

"Oh, Hermann has his use. But you also, my friend, are a very powerful man, and your intelligence makes the perfect combination for me that Hermann does not."

King filled his pipe very deliberately before he spoke. "A partnership, huh? What about your Sir Harry and your monkey food?"

"What if I told you there is no monkey food?"

King blew luxurious smoke from his pipe. "No news to me. You told me that when you said you might forget what it looked like, once you got here. And you told me something else right then, only you didn't know it—that you had a buried treasure here and you knew damn well if you came looking for financing for a treasure hunt you'd get the bum's rush. So you framed up this semi-scientific yarn that was new enough to catch your sucker. I'll hand it to you for a smart one."

"Oho! So you guessed that. You are smarter than I realized, my friend."

"Aw, not so much." King could not abide compliments. "I guessed at it pretty close and the witch doctor confirmed it."

"Ah! Just what did that witch doctor tell you?"

King pulled his nearly dead pipe to a thick mosquito smudge and said very coolly.

"Told me you swiped the juju."

Bentnick started visibly. "How could he tell you that?"

"Easy. Swiped a year ago. You were here a year ago. No white men here since. And this village, that has juju poles still standing, was deserted, from the looks of the growth, just about a year ago."

Bentnick was awed to a long silence. At last he said tightly:

"You know much indeed. Almost too much."

"Sure," King agreed cheerfully. "Almost everything. Only thing I don't know is where you buried it."

"Ah! So then I still have something to offer for a deal."

"On what basis?"

"Fifties. You and I."

"What's it worth?"

"I do not know. But—the One-Eyed Juju, you understand?"

King grunted. "So it was a case of plain loot, eh? The usual thing, I suppose? What was it? Diamond?"

"I think so." Bentinck's voice dropped at the drama of it. "As big as a pigeon egg! Only cemented in so hard, I had no time to get it out. The spears were close on my heels. We can get it—now—and get away in the canoe. We two."

"And Sir Harry? And your Hermie?"

The moon had come high enough to reveal the dim form by King's side. He could see it shrug.

"My dear friend! Dead weight. They can find their own way out of the mess. And if they are too stupid—" King could see the shoulders shrug beside him.

KING WAS not angry. Nobody could knock around Africa for long and not know that the world was full of all kinds of people with all kinds of ideas.

"Pally," he said calmly, "you just can't understands I got a job here to deliver His Nibs safe, and another job to keep *your* head off a juju pole just so an army won't come to avenge worthless white man blood. And besides that, there's my Masai and Hottentot here, and— Aw, hell. It's outside of your range."

Bentinck was encouraged by King's calmness into further argument.

"Do not worry about me, my friend, I have been here before and came out with my skin."

"When you got here they were friends. Dumb clucks thought a white man was white."

Bentinck snarled to offense. "Do not practice your talent for insult on me, my so tough friend. I am not Sir Jenks. But I still offer you opportunity for your help. What do all these others and your two black men weigh against the stake—the fortune— of two smart men in Africa?"

King drew it out to emphasis. "Black men. But *my men!* Shucks, it'd take too long to explain so you'd see any of it. You'll even hate to give up your loot, won't you? But I'm telling you, fella, you'll have to. Because that's going to be the only way out a lot of killings."

"Give up my—" Bentinck jumped from the log and faced King, hunched forward, ready. "But do not talk like a fool, you who pretend to dislike so much some killing. Before I give up I will—"

King billowed smoke. "You won't. Not even a pot shot out

of the dark. Because you need me to get you alive out of this mess that is so much worse than even you can realize."

Bentinck's right hand froze on his gun under his shirt; his left unconsciously went to feel the turn of his neck at the shoulder.

"Feeling kinda loose?" King could grin a sour satisfaction at that. "Well, just to ease your conscience so you can sleep, listen to those drums. Smart men in Africa ought to learn to read drums. I'm not that smart, but I know a war talk when I hear one. My bet is, by morning this place will be surrounded by a couple of thousand spearmen."

CHAPTER V

THE WORD OF SERKALI

THE FIRST glint of dawn showed that King was horribly right, for it glinted on bright metal all along the jungle fringe, waiting only for the ghosts to leave the haunted area.

"Guns!" King snapped. "Every gun in camp! You constables—catch any camp boys who have sense enough to hold one so it doesn't look like a broom and pass out the spares. Parade 'em around. Make a showing. And listen—" He directed his scowl particularly at the white men. "Blood spilled means retaliation, so get this very straight. Any fool who shoots before we have to—before I do—I'll put a bullet into him without batting an eye."

They could be seen now—dark forms behind every tree, some of them boldly in the open, not quite bold enough to be the first to start a rush against so many guns.

"As ugly a crowd as I've seen." King squinted narrow-eyed round the irregular tree wall, and scowled at Bentinck. "And they got a right to be. You know any prayers, just peel some off so they don't recognize you."

But Bentinck knew no prayers with that much power. They saw him, and the angry war cry lifted around the circle in the multi-toned baying of a pack that has run its long-sought quarry to earth. Some jumped up and down and howled their rage to the sky; the bolder ones made short little leaping rushes that needed only the support of a few to develop into a massed charge.

Bentinck's dry tongue ran across bloodless lips.

"You asked for it," King growled. "What d'you think these people are? Monkeys like your Hermie, to forget? Watch it, everybody! If they rush we'll just have to shoot it out."

The Masai knew his African psychology of personal challenge that holds with all primitive people. With superb arrogance he strode out and stalked in all his menacing nakedness within easy spear throw of the circle, stiff legged, like a lion daring the yapping lesser beasts, growling from his deep belly. Where a bold one leaped and yelled the loudest he poised, half crouched on wide splayed toes, and shook his great spear high.

"Who comes?" he called. "Who comes to talk with us twain—death and an Elmoran of the Masai? Which two come? Men to man, spear to spear? Which three come? *Hau!* Are there no warriors here?"

Sir Harry's inherent instincts rose to the magnificent drama of it. He even cheered.

"Oh, played!" he ejaculated. "Played indeed! Oh, cricket!"

The thought of concerted combat, uncertainly taking shape in the mob, swung back to the more primitive one of personal combat; but no warrior, nor any three, were jointly mad enough to offer themselves for sacrifice.

King caught Bentinck by the arm. "Quick! Parade your gorilla out! He can be useful for that much, anyhow."

Bentinck fired quick gutterals at Hermann. He understood and he was brave enough. He lumbered forward, swinging his huge axe in his hands and roaring his rage out of his great gash of a mouth.

The sheer brute size of him had its effect on the lesser humans, as Goliath affected the Israelites. Nor was any David to hand.

"Watch him!" King found a new anxiety. "Don't let him go berserk and start something. We've got them stopped for now."

M O B   R A G E frittered itself out in threatening demonstration. Men still howled and capered with spears, but the thought of a concerted rush was broken, and as the morning moved on to hot noon the loudest demonstrators squatted in the tree shade. Only occasionally some resentful warrior's anger burst in a sporadic leap and a yell. A leader, clearly, was needed to work the pack up again to killing fury.

At the exact hour of noon a commotion indicated that a leader was forthcoming. A confusion of yells in the deep jungle drew slowly nearer, until it concentrated at the fringe. Then a man stepped into the open and a surge of men howled out behind him to form a rugged black baseboard to the green tree wall.

A portentous figure of a man. Buffalo horns were ponderous on his head. His eyes were daubed with white circles like a circus clown's. A monkey skull made a grinning pendant on his chest. Dried embryos and bones made up a phantasmagoria of gruesome costume.

"*Ai-we!*" the Hottentot chattered. "A witch-doctor! Here will the spear of wit be needed that may avert that of steel."

The man walked forward, confidently alone, without showing any nervousness.

Bentinck's thought was instant. "Grab him for a hostage and we'll be able to bargain."

King snapped, "Don't talk like a fool. Savages have no more inhibitions than you. What would a hostage's life weigh against a feud vengeance?"

"If you know so much—"

"Shut up! Get your gorilla. And you, Sir Harry. The three of you guard around the other side of the clearing so nobody jumps us. I'll go out and talk to this guy."

In the no man's land, just beyond the edge of spear throw, they met.

The man gave the greeting amicably enough. "*Jambo, Mzungu.*" He studied King with searching black eyes as keen as a crow's. In spite of his fantastic make-up, King could see that the man was certainly a leader who could influence men. The face beneath the paint was savagely strong and more than savagely intelligent.

"Yes," the man nodded to his scrutiny of King. "You will be the white man of whom the word came."

He spoke with the curiously compressed lips of a man who is practiced in ventriloquism.

"Ha!" King guessed immediately. "The head priest of the juju! This'll be a tough one."

The man said in a chanting monotone, as though recalling a dim message, imperfectly received; "The word said that a white man comes who is the friend of Great Ones, who understands the ways of our people, who knows how to deal with honor and justice with those who have the wisdom."

King knew perfectly well that he referred to his brother wizard, but he deliberately misinterpreted it.

"Yes. I come from the greatest in the land. I represent the *Serkali,* the Government."

Without expression the head priest said: "There are those of the *Serkali Beritishi* who understand nothing of the ways of our people. Yet you, who understand, will give us justice." Expression flared into his face, savage exultation. He shot out an open hand to point, fingers clawed in demand. "That man is ours, for an offering to the ghost of our juju whom he stole!"

King flashed a look and saw that Bentinck and Hermann had deserted their post and crept up behind him. His own anger flared as savagely, almost, as the priest's.

"Damn you. I told you to guard the rear."

Bentinck's tongue was licking his dry teeth.

"I'm in on this. He is talking about me, isn't he?"

King couldn't argue with him then. He turned back to the juju priest with the ever unsatisfactory promise:

"Justice will be dealt to this man by the *Serkali*."

IT SATISFIED the savage crowd no more than the same promise ever satisfied a lynching mob. The juju doctor shouted refusal and flung his both arms wide, working himself up to declamatory fury.

"What is a justice to us that we cannot see and will be judged leniently by men who have lost nothing? The evil was done here and here it must be judged and paid!"

The hum of his people behind him was like darkly massed bees.

Essentially the argument was sound enough—that a criminal be taken back to the district of his crime for judgment. For the moment King had no argument to advance.

Bentinck was muttering rapid translations to Hermann. Hermann's breath was snorting like a bull buffalo's rage mounting.

The priest declaimed further, "We have no quarrel with the *Serkali* to make a war with it, for we have seen war. Yet the crime has been great and the payment overdue."

Rhetoric was working up the mob. Its low thunder rumbled again round the horizon.

"We have no quarrel against the servant of the *Serkali*. Therefore we will send you, *Mzungu*, back to the *Serkali* with gifts to explain to those who do not understand that we take the payment that is here in our hands."

King had no logical reason to offer against that claim. Only once again the unsatisfactory baldness of dogged statement.

"The *Serkali* will do justice."

"Did the white *Serkali* do justice a year ago for this white man's evil? Moreover, having escaped justice once, when he comes again with more white men and guns, does he bring good? Or does he bring more evil? Tell me that, *Mzungu*. Tell it aloud so that the people may hear."

A savagely shrewd debater was the man, and the strength of his argument was that he demanded vengeance exactly as any white mob does. Their leader's unanswerable logic fed raw adrenalin into the blood of his warriors. They leaped high again, howling, and the tap of spear on shield was a rattle of impending fight.

"Therefore," the priest screamed, and he reached past King, "we take these three white men now, to make them ghosts to serve the ghost of our juju."

His clutching hand almost reached Bentinck. Bentinck flung himself back to roll on the ground. From there he spat commands to Hermann, who lurched forward, his great axe heaved high.

The priest's rhetoric broke in a falsetto screech of fear and he turned in a desperate run.

Hermann would have split him like a mutton.

But King shot out a foot and tripped him.

Hermann sprawled on his face, half winded by the force of his own mighty rush. The priest scuttled back to the shelter of his massed people, all of them suddenly agape and momentarily frozen in their action by a violence that had forestalled their own.

"You blasted fool!" Bentinck shrieked. "That would have shown them. Why didn't you let—"

In the confusion of those tense few seconds another confusion broke at the opposite end of the clearing. A surging and yelling of men. A shout from Sir Harry. A yelp from the Hottentot.

"They have him, *Bwana!*"

KING RACED to the other side of the standing huts in

time to see the white of Sir Harry's drill jacket disappearing amongst the trees, hustled along by a swarm of black men.

His rifle snapped to his shoulders, but he held it so, his finger tense on the trigger. After the jacket was out of sight he lowered it slowly, the muzzle of it swinging to the shake of his head.

"No. They'd spear him at the first shot."

A triumphant yelling showed that the savages were hustling their first captive round to the juju priest.

The only dim spark of compensation out of that calamity was that it, combined with the priest's sudden discomfiture, had once again broken the rising impulse to mob action. A breathing spell.

Bentinck's quick mind was not empty of ideas, whatever his terror.

"If we can hold them off until night, we could get away—in the dark, while they are afraid of ghosts. You and I, my friend. We could slip through."

"*We?*" King cuffed Bentinck with his open hand across the side of his face and sent him reeling. "Damn your soul, I can walk out of this trap any time I want to pick up my hat. You heard him. But I've got to get that other worthless hulk out of here."

He stamped over to where the native camp boys huddled, saucer-eyed, muttering to one another to boost their courage that all this was an affair of the white men alone. He called his own men aside. The angles of his face stood out very grim.

"Listen well. There is no time for argument. Immediate action is necessary before they get entirely out of hand. I must go and bring that man back."

There was no argument.

"Yes, *Bwana*," the Masai said in simple agreement. "It is for our honor. It will be a snatching of meat from between the very teeth of death. Yet we must."

The great fellow's simple loyalty dissipated all of King's anger and left only the grimness. He put his brown hand on the black shoulder to give it a little shake.

"Not we, old warrior. Not this time. This is a thing that I must do alone. Or at least—" He searched the faces of the two native constables—"with other help."

The constables stood his thin gaze with African stolidity. Slowly King told them: "The chief Hawkes said you *askaris* would follow to the death."

They both said it together. "Our lives are already once owing to Bwana."

The commotion and shouting in the jungle had worked its way around to where the priest stood. His group yelled triumph and brandished spears.

Bentinck edged into it. "What crazy thing are you planning to do? My God, man! If you go near them and some mad buck stabs you, that will be the signal. They will come in a wave."

King paid no attention to him. He was muttering to himself in narrow-eyed rumination: "Damn it, if they can do it, I can do it. White man juju. Well, sometimes it works."

He nodded to the Hottentot. "Go on, Kaffa. Get it. In my blanket roll." He told the constables: "You will carry your rifles. At shoulder, as guard. There will be no chance to use them, anyhow."

He swung his own rifle off his shoulder and gave it to the Masai.

"Don't know much about this," he growled, "but I've an idea an officer doesn't carry one."

Kaffa came with the uniform coat that he had accepted so derisively from Hawkes. King squeezed into it.

Bentinck caught at his arm. "Good God! Don't do it! We have only you to rely on to get us out of this."

"Shut up," King flared at him. "I've got something else here that you'll never understand. Something that these stiff-necked British know how to build. White man prestige!"

Bentinck clung to him.

"Barounggo," King told the Massai evenly, "if any—accident—happens, spear me this man first."

"Yes, *Bwana.* There will also be a vengeance before we follow."

"Come on, you two *askaris.* March."

KING STEPPED slowly toward the milling herd at the jungle fringe, only his pistol in his holster. If the mob went mad, he knew a pistol would be of no more practical use than a rifle. This was a condition that called for a something more subtle and, in the long run, much more potent than bullets.

The uniform coat strangled his shoulders. He lifted his elbows and hunched sharply. The coat ripped up the back seam, but the front still glittered with its buttons. The two uniformed constables slopped behind him in their bare feet.

It called for nerve, but white men had done it before. It called for the kind of cold nerve that had put white men on top in Africa. It called for a lot of other things too—duty, patriotism, service. King didn't know anything about those others. He kept muttering to himself: "If any Limey's got the gall, damn it, I got it."

The yelping warriors stopped their capering to stare at the portent of the tall white man stepping slowly right at them, without fanfare or gesticulation, his big shoulders hunched, his face thrust grimly forward.

Those nearest to his advance shuffled on their feet and edged back into the support of their fellows. Their fellows edged away. A little lane opened. Through it King could see the priest and a mob holding on to their prisoner with as many hands as could touch him.

King stepped into the black lane of bodies. The constables slopped after him. The rank sweat of animal anger was heavy in the breezeless air.

A tall fellow yelled in sudden frenzy and heaved up a spear before King's face.

King looked at the man, not so steadily as to lift the thing to the importance of a contest of wills.

"Down, fool!" he told him. "I talk with your chief."

The spear point touched King's chest, the staring eyes hot behind it. King put it aside with a slow, grave, movement and went on through. The savage stared after him, still holding his spear suspended in empty air.

The juju priest stared levelly into King's eyes. King didn't attempt anything so theatrical as to stare him down. His eyes were narrow on the witch doctor's and his mouth twisted, more annoyed than angry. He said:

"Your foolish young man makes much unnecessary trouble for me. For I now come to take this man back."

Sir Harry Jenk's white face, even the mottles drained of blood, stared from over woolly heads at the enormity of King's confidence.

The head priest said: "Many spears grow in the path that leads back."

King didn't turn to look at the spears. He said: "Only spears as foolish as the *mwitu* weed grow in the path of the *Serkali* before the *Serkali* tramples them down, as you, who have seen war, know."

Grunts and muttered assent came in little sporadic explosions from others who had seen war. The juju doctor, as quick as any white leader to sense his people's reaction, was quick to turn on another tack. He quoted the native version of a familiar problem.

"The lean meat in a man's hand is more valuable than the fat buck that runs. If the *Serkali* values this man, we will make a good offer. We will exchange him for that evil one who is worthless."

The warriors exploded in fierce unanimity to that.

"It is a good offer," said King. "Were I alone, I would accept it. But the *Serkali's* honor values that man to do justice on him."

The juju priest flared angrily to his old argument that his people understood. "What is a justice so far away that the people who have suffered the evil cannot see it?"

King's chest, for the first time, was able to draw in a full breath. He was able, even, to show a thin pinching of his lips. Argument, rather than bloody action, was the first thin wedge of persuasion. The grin was very thin, very grim in its tentative promise.

"That you should see the justice, can perhaps be arranged."

The warrior mob yelled and stood literally on tiptoes to get the significance of that. The juju doctor searched King's face for possible trickery.

"How can it be arranged, *Mzungu,* since the *Serkali* is far? Words do not pay for restitution. The luck of my people has been evil ever since our juju went. Its ghost must be appeased before we are whole again."

The grin was almost a thin slit.

"Even the change of your luck might be arranged—after I have taken this white man back."

The priest stared uncompromisingly at King.

"On whose word, *Mzungu?* Do you promise the word of the *Serkali?*"

There was the old unsatisfactory deadlock on the question of a far away authority.

King took a momentous gamble. He was gambling with men's lives anyhow. He shook his head and he called his bet aloud so that everybody could hear it.

"Not on the word of the far away *Serkali.* On my own word, who am here. The word of the Bwana Kingi, about whom the talk came that he deals justly with those who have wisdom."

Indecision was on the head priest's face and his people's. It must be done now, or the gamble was a bad bet and the spears would take the odds.

King took a long step forward, past the priest, pushed aside black bodies whose minds left them wavering, and put his hand on Sir Harry Jenks. He barked brisk orders.

"Loose him there, you. Come on, quick about it. Talk is now finished. My word is given. We go."

IT WAS like taking meat from a hungry pack. Spear points were at King's breast, at his back—worse, at his stomach, pricking through the cloth against his skin until he could feel the quiver of the muscles that held them, waiting for a tremor of an eyelash, a false move, an incautious word.

King didn't look at the spears. He looked only at the fierce faces above them. He did not know how grimly, fiercely his own face looked down at the ring of watching eyes.

Slowly the grasping hands let go. Slowly a lane opened before King's confident advance. Slowly—so slowly as to seem nonchalant—King walked through it. Sir Harry came like a man stunned. The constables fell stolidly in and slopped behind in their bare feet.

Five paces! Ten! The grin that had been trying to break through for so long cracked thinly. He said to Sir Harry, "Does the small of your back feel as crawly as mine—*don't* look back!"

Twenty measured paces! Sir Harry's exclamation exploded from him. "By Jove!"

Ten more paces! Struggling words poured from Sir Harry.

"Magnificent, Sir! Splendidly done indeed! I, er—apologize and all that. And—thanks. That took courage, sir. I would like to shake your hand."

Out of spear range! Only confused murmurs of milling men behind, resentful still of what they had lost, uncertain of what to do about it.

The Masai put the practical aspect of the thing forward, simply, without any extravagance of words.

"Our honor will be very great amongst these people, *Bwana*."

"As also of these two *askaris*, whom the Bwana Hawkes will promote for this."

Bentinck, his face twitching still, stared at King as at something utterly beyond any hope of understanding. King's strain broke to release some more of its tension on him. He levelled an accusing finger at him and told him mercilessly:

"And don't you ever imagine, when they get you, that I'll ever come after you. They can spread-eagle you on juju poles—and watch me laugh."

Out of the swelling murmurs behind came the juju doctor's call, almost as though timed to the climax.

"But there will be no escape, white men. Justice must be delivered. Many spears fence this place."

"You hear that?" King looked around at the approaching dusk musingly. "Though I suppose a fellow *could* get away in the dark."

He turned away from Bentinck and hid his shameless grin. "Well, we're out of trouble for today, anyhow. Guess we can sleep in peace tonight, and for myself I'll say I need it."

It was well into the night, therefore, when the late moon was at last up, that the Hottentot woke King.

"*Bwana.* They move softly in their hut."

King was up immediately. "Ha! Just what I figured. Call Barounggo. We wait and follow."

Within a few minutes the lithe form of Bentinck and the lumbering one of Hermann stole out of their hut and crept across the clearing to the path that came in from the river.

"What now, *Bwana?*" Barounggo asked. "Do we let them escape?"

King was grinning in very self satisfied anticipation. "No. But unless my bet is away off, we're on our way to get the one-eyed juju."

No outcry came from the path, no murmur of excited spearmen. The encircling hordes were content to stay well away from the haunted area. Like ghosts themselves the three followed the sounds of the two.

"Yet have a care," King warned. "That one is no fool."

"As cunning as an ant pig," the Hottentot agreed. "Yet that great '*Ngagi* of his tramples like a buffalo." He chucked impish recollection. "*E-we, Bwana.* This is better than when we followed him in just such a path and thought he was a ghost."

A few minutes further he stopped, balanced on one foot, the other frozen in Mid-Action like a bird dog.

"*Bwana*, the '*Ngagi* makes no sound, but the clever one's feet go on."

"Ho!" King growled. "Clever enough to have spotted us, and leaves the gorilla to hold us off while he grabs the loot and runs. Careful now, Apeling. That great one is not so foolish as he pretends."

Presently the Hottentot stopped again, sniffing. "*Bwana*, this is my thought. That great tree beside the path where the moon comes through; he waits behind it to slay who walk unsuspecting into the light."

T H E J U N G L E was a dense wall on either side. Impossible to creep around on the man, even though they might think that the three of them might disarm the murderous giant. And the soft sounds of Bentinck's passage were growing fainter.

"Thus we do, *Bwana*." The Hottentot was all eager to retrieve a disgrace that had overwhelmed him in a very similar circumstance. "I will creep close and leap through the lit space, thus drawing his stroke. Once he has frightened me, but not again."

Before King could stop him the little imp had scuttled forward. A moment he paused before the tree, deliberately made a noise, and then scooted out through the shimmery trap.

On his very heels the great axe blade, that must have been held high in vicious anticipation, swished down and buried itself in the earth in a stroke that would have split the Hottentot like a banana.

Again, before King could stop him, the Masai bounded forward. Like the Hottentot, he too, harbored a fierce shame.

He bounded over the axe as it tugged free of the ground. But unlike the Hottentot, he didn't race on into the farther dark.

He turned and stood in the full moonlight, poised on his splayed toes, crouched and growling.

It all happened so quickly that King could take no hand.

Hermann's murderous rage roared from him. King, still on the other side of the tree, saw the great axe glitter in a tremendous horizontal sweep aimed at the Masai's naked waist; saw the Masai, with all the superb skill of a bullfighter, shrink his stomach back just the necessary inches to avoid it; saw him lunge in and upwards with his spear.

King raced on down the path. Bentinck's foot steps had faded away. King, in a frenzy of imminent failure, forced himself to stop and listen.

If Bentinck, too, had not been in a frenzy of haste, if he had been normally cunning, King would never have heard him. But the sound came. A splashing of water from the river.

He crashed through to the sound and came on Bentinck, waist deep in the water, struggling with a dark object that was too heavy to be easily lifted clear of its water support. King saw the flash of Bentinck's knife in the moonlight, poking at the thing, as he jumped on him.

Bentinck screamed.

"Sure you'd have sunk it." King had him by his neck and his knife arm. "Easy enough to dope it out you'd have no time for anything else. But nobody could search the whole muddy river."

Bentinck babbled curses and pleas and promises all at once. "You blasted fool! Let me dig it out! It's worth a fortune—both our fortunes. Leave the damned idol. We can get away light."

"No you don't, my smart fool. That eye belongs right where it is. And a lot of people's lives worth more'n yours hinge on it."

Bentinck wrenched his arm free and stabbed at King's chest. King beat him to the punch, inside of his arm, fair and hard in his throat. The knife ripped the back of King's shoulder and dropped from Bentinck's fingers.

King whistled softly to signal to his men.

MORNING GLINTED again on spears, stubbornly massed round the clearing, thicker than before, since warriors from outlying villages had come to close the cordon.

King breakfasted leisurely and lit his pipe. Then he told the Masai:

"All right, Barounggo. Make the proclamation."

The Masai strutted forth before the people. His spear was polished until the smooth hard wood of it reflected light like its blade. His shield was a newly painted splendor in the sun. His elbow and knee garters of monkey hair were combed. He filled his chest and boomed forth the fantastic *bonga* titles that he invented for his master.

"The Bwana Kingi speaks through my mouth. Kingi *mkubwa*, who has lent honor to the *Serkali* by for a short time serving it. *Mkubwa ma-hila*, the Great Wise One who smells out evil— *Mwinda ya ndhovu*, the hunter of elephants—*baba wa simba*, the father of lions. Hear therefore, you little people and bow your heads."

The Masai loved it. His African sense of flamboyant drama revelled in the sheer theater of it. The people who heard loved it.

"All right, all right," King said from behind. "Get on with it."

The Masai was disappointed. He could have recited *bonga* for half an hour. He would have to reserve it for the later telling, when those same people would make a feast for him.

"The Bwana Kingi, who gave a word that even the *Serkali* could not give, now makes his word good. He delivers justice. He brings recompense. He—"

"All right, Kaffa. Bring him out." King cut it short.

The Hottentot came from a hut, leading a rope. Behind him staggered Bentinck. Bentinck followed perforce because the other end of the rope swathed him and the burden on his back. The object was not much bigger than an organ, a chunky, squat thing of stone blackened by years of blood sacrifice that had been spilled over it.

The Hottentot led him forward. The massed warriors goggled at the portent, silent, mouths open. By some sort of telepathic communication their wonder flashed itself round the wide flung circle of spears. All gabble ceased. Those in front backed away before the advance. Only the juju doctor came forward.

King grinned at him. "So is my word made good. He who did the evil makes restitution. He who stole it brings it back."

The priest said three words. "*Bwana*"—Not *Mzungu*— "*Bwana mkubwa mema!*" And he snatched the ragged blanket from the Hottentot's shoulders and flung it over his juju and its bearer to hide them from sacrilegious eyes.

Bentinck screamed.

"Wait a minute," King said to the priest. "Not so fast—not yet." And to Bentinck he said grimly: "Your last chance, feller. Come out of your sulk now and talk. There's only the one thing I don't know about this business. How did you build your Hermie up so strong in six years? Talk or, by God, I'll turn you and your load over in one piece."

Bentinck talked. Sulkily still, but he told his secret.

"The photograph was his brother."

"Ha!" Enlightenment burst from King. "Smart trick, by golly! That's the only one I couldn't dope out. Smart fella like you ought to have made more profit out of Africa than you're going to."

He said to the priest: "Thus the man makes restitution. But the man was not in the word that I gave. Your juju is yours, and brings back with it the luck that it took away. The man goes back with me for a justice yet to be done on him by the *Serkali*. It is a good offer."

The juju doctor did not bargain. He said: "It is a good offer. I alone speak for all my people. We take it. Between my people and the *Serkali* that delivers justice there is no war."

"Which," King said with a grim dryness, "saves your people a lot more grief than you know about. Okay, Kaffa. Cut him loose."

Sir Harry sat on the great flat-topped log beside King and

listened to the demoniac frenzy of midnight drums. They were alone. All the camp had gone to the feast. Sir Harry said:

"So we learn by experience, eh what? I have learned a few things about our African colony that more of our administrators ought to know. I shall invite some of them to be my guests on another safari next season, and, er—old man, I'd like to engage you in advance to take charge of operations and teach them. That is, of course, if Captain Hawkes will release you."

"Guess I'm released already," King grinned. "Listen to that jamboree out there. My chore was only to see that those naked savages didn't make a whole lot of trouble for themselves. As for teaching, it was the jungle taught you. It has brought people down to earth before."

Sir Harry amended that. "The jungle and, ah—Kingi Bwana. So, if you would—what I mean, some of my lordly friends have taken occasion to make sure that I should recognize their inherited superiority. So if you could—just for the good of their aristocratic souls—bring them down to earth with a little hardy insult, don't you know."

"Me?" said King. "Hell, I never insult anybody. Never told you any but the raw truth, did I?"

"Well, no, you didn't," Sir Harry admitted. "But a little raw truth would be awf'ly good for some of them."

"I'm hired," King said. "Only I'll hate to take your money for teaching the raw truth about Africa to your lordlings."

"For the good of the Empire." Sir Harry excused his plot with the national slogan.

"Empire hell," said King. "For the good of poor saps like Hawkes and Tommy Ansell and me, who come and make a tough living here."

BLOOD AND STEEL

KING, TRADER, white hunter, and thorn in the side of many foolish people, pushed his tawny head up over the steep lip of the donga and paused with instinctive and quite unconscious caution to let his narrowed eyes first take a survey of every thing that moved on the plain.

"Anything—" It was an unshakable slogan of his—"can happen in Africa." And Kingi Bwana of the wide experience was just now being careful.

The thing that was happening a scant mile away was a startling verification of even so all embracing a slogan. What moved on the plain, a black dot in the distance still, was the most vicious live thing in Africa, and its quarry was a white man.

King heaved the rest of his sinewy length over the donga's edge and stood up, the better to see, while he sibilated the bitter Swahili proverb with his sharply drawn breath.

"The broken spear is needed a hundred times daily."

That was why King had been traveling along the bottom of the donga instead of wide open and don't-give-a-damn on the plain—because his weapon, his rifle, was broken.

He was climbing out of the donga because its precipitous sides were pinching in on him and he could see, only a hundred yards ahead, where a cascade of shale rubble marked the sudden narrow beginning of the erosion gully.

King turned his head for a moment from the desperate race

that thudded over the plain to call down the donga's depth: "Up, there! Quick and look!"

A Masai ostrich plume bobbed up; brawny limbs sprawled over the edge. The man reached a hand down and with a single long swing slung out of the depths a wizened little Hottentot who landed with simian agility on his feet and immediately hopped high again in excitement and shrilled a call, for all the world like a grass monkey.

The Masai stood to his height and looked. He exclaimed, "*Whau!*" Immediately then his iron calm asserted itself and he viewed the racing drama of life and death with impartial criticism.

"*Kifaru* pursues furiously, for, see his tail, he is much enraged; and I think indeed he will catch that motor car, for the driver is inexpert over this grass land."

King pulled his pith helmet low over his eyes to cut the upper glare and frowned narrowly at the advancing spectacle. For the moment the car was holding its own; a none too new model, it clangored and roared its laboring best. Behind it pounded the rhinoceros, nearly as big and quite as heavy and virulently more destructive than a car at its worst, snorting and blowing almost as loud.

AT THAT, steel and machinery ought to have outrun flesh and bone; only that the driver was woefully inexperienced over that kind of terrain. The car lurched over high tussocks of the stiff bunch grass, swayed drunkenly into the in-between depressions, jarred into clumps that visibly checked it before it could roar again to its pick-up. The thundering brute behind, born to that ground, was gaining.

"Tch-sha-a-ah!" King exhaled his impotent aggravation. Hard-boiled he was and attuned to African grimness, but his white man sensibilities had never learned to equal the Masai's African impersonality. "Why can't he pick the soft spots? Crack an axle or dish a wheel—any least thing happen, he'll be mush.

*The broad spear
had stabbed
down.*

That brute will knock his machine apart like a bomb and
trample him out all sticky."

His hands with automatic habit inched up to the ready position for snapping gun to shoulder. Then he swore helplessly
and let them drop. "And not a gun within a hundred miles!"

The driver saw the three human figures outlined against the
farther heat haze. Humans, therefore human aid! The impulse

was instinctive. He wrenched desperately at his wheel and headed directly for them.

And King—perhaps *the* man in all Africa most sure of stopping a charging rhino—weaponless! That was the grim humor of Africa.

"Wo-we!" The big Masai spat calmly. "The fool's fate reaches its appointed end. He will never see this donga in time and will plunge to the depth."

"Having first lured destruction upon all of us." The Hottentot danced and chattered abuse. "From a fool can his foolishness not be beaten with sticks." The proverb was amazingly like one recorded into Holy Writ by a man much wiser than he.

King jumped high, waved his arms and pointed wide sweeping gestures over to his right, beyond where the donga began its abrupt course.

The driver, fool though they all named him, retained sense enough in his extremity to understand the obvious signal. He wrenched his wheel over again and the car shuddered on in its altered career.

"Yet *Kifaru* will surely catch him," the Masai said, as callously as a white man watching greyhounds course a hare. The course paralleled them now—the car careened some two hundred yards away; the remorseless rhino pounded seventy yards behind.

"He avoids the new danger," said the Masai, "only to be overtaken by the old."

Much of the grief that came to King in Africa was because he was just not hard-boiled enough to stay out of trouble that was not strictly his own.

"Not so," he said quickly to the Masai. "For you can still divert *Kifaru* and haply snatch that man's life from his fate."

"*Wah, Bwana!*" The Masai's exclamation was one that could indicate surprise, or with almost the same intonation, indignation. His long oblique eyes judged distances as critically as they counted the chances of the grim race. "It might indeed be done, *Bwana.* But the life of a fool, is it worthy of the risk?"

It was quite impossible to drag eyes away from that race. King grated words only out of the corner of his mouth to his henchman.

"It is not an order, for death rides close on that play. Yet I would count it a favor."

"*Veme!*" The Masai shrugged further argument from his great shoulders. "Death and I have played many times together. I go."

"To this side of the donga," King called after him. "That the car may escape beyond."

THE MASAI ran with the swallow-like gliding motion of long limbed men whose legs are well muscled under their weight; his black ostrich plumes flattened back in the wind, the colobus monkey tail garters at his elbows and knees flickering like whips; his spear extended, he shouted as he ran the hoarse "*Ss-sghee*" of the Masai charge. A superb figure of savage daring.

"Ow-woo!" the Hottentot moaned. "All for a man who is a fool."

King knew to exactness what the Masai dared. He stood on wide-spread legs, his thumbs in his belt, twisting till the stout leather creaked.

The Masai raced on a diagonal slant to get between car and pursuing beast. The grass was as high as his knees, yet his feet seemed to skim the flattened tops.

"Ha!" It crackled from King. "He's cut the brute off!" An astounding term to apply to two hundred pounds of man opposed to two tons of furious beast. Yet there was the Masai leaping high and yelling full and fair in its path.

The death that he so familiarly scouted rode now on the chances of how soon the short-sighted brute might see him.

"The wind at least blows from him to it," the Hottentot moaned.

And it was scent, probably, rather than sight that checked

the beast's charge. It lurched suddenly to a stop. Its lowered head, long aimed at the car, flung up; its hair-fringed ears twitched; its little red-brown eyes peered to follow its nose. The horn of it stood up against the sky like a dark yard of threatening sword.

The Masai flung arms and legs wide to the air and leaped before it, yelling. A bare thirty paces before it, but enough.

"Ha!" It came dry and harsh from King again. "He's done it! Good man! Get ready, Apeling, to scramble down faster than ever you came up."

The rhino's insensate rage was immediately diverted to this new annoyance that pranced before it. It snorted a staccato succession of small explosions, down-horned again and lumbered forward to obliterate the annoyance.

A cool man with steel nerves, armed with a rifle, could then have fired over the tip of the horn into the brute's brain. A desperate man with steel spring sinews, armed with only a spear and having no other recourse, might possibly have dodged aside and driven his blade into the comparatively soft skin under the beast's foreleg. A skilled and very powerful spearman might— just barely possibly—have so killed it. The thing had been done in Africa.

The Masai, haply, was not that desperate. The donga was his better recourse. He yelled once again and turned and sped back, winging over the grass tops like a dark swooping bird, the darker mass of snorting hate behind him.

"Ha!" said King. "He's safe!" He was all unconscious of the enormity of applying the term to the appalling circumstance. "Down you go, little ape, and up the other side fast, lest the beast sees the donga no better than the car and crashes down on us."

The Hottentot was already scuttling down. King swung his legs over, felt for toe holds, found root grips, reached the bottom with an avalanche of red clay dirt. He sprang across and was nearly to the top on the other side when he heard the hard pad-pad of the Masai's feet. Then he saw him.

Like a great dark bird again. Arms wide, garter fringes flapping, legs drawn high to his belly, sailing over. All of an eighteen foot leap. Nothing for an athlete taking off from a hard packed surface with a white line to mark the spot; but from the uneven lip of a ravine a very nice little job of jumping.

Then he saw the rhino, appallingly close and monstrous, looming black like a locomotive. Saw it suddenly stiffen its squat forelegs; saw the horny great pads of its feet plow twin deep furrows in the soil that immediately hid it in red dust as thick as the swirling haze of his own hurried passage across the donga.

He listened, rather than looked, for the shuddering impact of four thousand pounds on the donga's bottom. The moment passed. No impact came. Then he looked to see that his Hottentot was safe.

Safe enough and vociferous. The little man danced on the ravine lip in vituperative derision, waiting only for the dust to float clear enough for his triumph of safety. He prepared himself by tearing clods of earthy sod from the ground and chattering curses that there were no stones.

The dust thinned. The great brute looked at the chasm before it and blew vast breaths of steam. It tossed its head in perplexity, suddenly very much like a horse in its reactions.

The Hottentot spat on a clod of turf.

"This, Black One, is my blessing," he shouted and flung it to powder off the beast's armor plated side.

The beast muttered explosively and kicked forward with its great toes.

"This, O offal of cave spirits," the Hottentot yelled again, "is the blessing of my father and of all his forty-three children."

The clod shattered over the beast's face. It drove its great horn deep into the ground and plowed barrow loads of turf at a time; it stamped upon them, squealing.

The Hottentot, spat upon each succeeding clod in the copied Masai custom of imparting blessing. "This, pig with a diseased nose, is the well wishing of my whole tribe."

The Masai stood in immense dignity. He said. "Look, *Bwana.* It is no wonder that the beast is enraged."

King looked at it with a thin frown. "Poor devil."

From its left shoulder protruded the broken haft of a spear, fixed there because the blade must have turned on itself like an iron claw.

"The man," said the Masai impassively, "was a brave one and the stroke almost in the exact spot; though were it I, I would have aimed a shade forward. A pity that the steel was not worthy of the man."

King shook his head. "A pity it is that so much shoddy material gets traded around to naked men who have a man's courage but the sense of children. That man's village will be one for the trader to keep away from, if he wants to keep on living."

And then at last he had time to remember the Masai's superb stunt.

"It was well done, Barounggo. A man's deed. It will be remembered. That man's life you surely saved to be counted against the many you have taken."

"*Whau, Bwana!*" The Masai's viewpoint was extraordinarily practical. "It remains yet to be seen whether the saving was worth the man."

ABOVE THE snorting and raging of the rhinoceros before them came the snorting and clanking of the car from behind. All three men turned appraising eyes upon the occupant, whom they knew so far only as a man lamentably unfamiliar with that country.

"At least," the Masai said, "his limbs are not stiffened with fear of the death that followed."

The car clattered to a stand. The man in it leaned out to show a square face young and ruddy with the frost chapping of England's winter. Whether he grinned out of one side of his mouth or whether the distortion was caused by a monocle that lifted that half of his face was not clear. He said:

"The brute's pretty demmed shirty, what?"

King looked him over with a face as expressionless as though it was hewn out of hard-grained wood. He was never one to expand to a meaningless smile upon the mere approach of another white man, and anger he never let an enemy see. He said:

"Shirty, as you say, and then some."

"Come jolly near to getting me, too." The young man shivered a little.

"And still might," King said. "Come along—keep moving down donga. It'll be twenty miles before it'll flatten out enough for any rhino to get across, and with any luck it'll be too dumb to go around the upper end. Keep slinging mud at Kifaru, Kaffa, and lure him along a ways."

"By Jove!" The young man showed alarm. "D'you really think, old man, it might get it into its head to come round?"

"It could. Anything can happen if the gods of Africa decide they don't want somebody on their landscape. Keep moving."

The car lurched along. On the other side of the donga, so close that you could see the hate in its little pig eyes, the rhino paralleled it, kicking huge divots of sod at intervals, slashing its horn through the earth with a grunt and a vast heave.

The destructive potentiality of the thing was appalling.

"By Jove!" The man showed anxiety. "What that would do to a car!"

"Don't worry," King reassured him. "If it decided to come around the short end we'd just climb down and up the other side again. But you'd sure see a nice fast job of car wrecking."

The man positively shuddered alarm. "But that's just it. I dashed well can't afford to have him wreck my car."

"Oh," said King. "The car?" King's face indicated that what-ever the fellow's other shortcomings, he was not to be condemned for cold feet. "Well, keep it moving," he said. "We'll be edging away in a while and let the brute forget us."

The maneuver was simple enough. Lured along beyond all chance of remembering that the car of its original hate must have found a way available to itself, the brute still tossed dust in the distance and nursed an abiding rage that forgot all immediate cause but remained ready to destroy immediately anything else that it might see.

"By the way," the young man shouted, "my name's Ponsonby."

King flicked a hand in acknowledgment.

"King," he shouted back.

The name meant nothing to Ponsonby. The fact was an indication that he knew nothing at all about British East Africa. Out of which the mystery remained—what in the name of all that was harebrained was he doing there alone in his ignorance? King stalked on; he was not interested enough in any Ponsonby to ask.

Ponsonby broke another clanking silence. "I say, old man. That was awf'ly sporting, what?"

"What?" King shouted back.

"I mean this big Johnny of yours with the spear. Most sporting thing a fellow ever saw—I kept looking back, you know. I've an idea the fellow saved my life."

"He did." King smiled briefly. "The two of them behind us are debating now whether the saving was worth while."

"Oh, I say! Come now!" Ponsonby's wide eyes let go of his monocle. It was only after a long rattling period that he was able to shout, "Rum beggars, these Africans."

KING STALKED on, uncompromising, his eyes searching the uneven plain for a place to camp. He picked the most uncomfortable spot in a radius of three miles, a low *kloof*, a rocky outcrop of tumbled great boulders. "Where rhino's don't come charging along," was his laconic explanation. But he added, "Your car, not moving, will be safe."

"Dry camp and tight belts," he said casually. "Unless, that is, you're heeled."

"You mean, tucker, old man? Why certainly. I'm er—equipped, if that's what you mean. But—" Ponsonby had a more urgent matter on his mind—"this chappie of yours. I'm obliged to him no end. I don't suppose I could offer to pay him, could I? What I mean, looks like a sort of a gentleman, if you know what I mean."

King's appraisal of Ponsonby's shortcomings allowed his lips to crack to a visible grin. "I give you credit for perception," he said, but Ponsonby didn't know what he meant. "But you might say 'thank you'. And they're practical folks. Africans; a small gift would show you meant it."

"Certainly. Least I could do." Ponsonby ran to his car and came back with a shiny new *panga,* a machete sort of knife that East Africans use for just about every purpose from whittling toothpicks to building a house.

Barounggo accepted it gravely.

"Tell the white man it is a great gift for a small service," he said formally, but while he said it he was holding it suspended below the wooden grip. He applied his thumb nail to the edge and snapped away to test its ring. The blade gave out a dull *pung* instead of the clear, vibrating *ping-g-g,* that is prized. "But tell him," the Masai said with uncompromising African practical- ity, "that the steel is worthless."

King spared Ponsonby a literal translation of that. But he credited him with the appreciative thought behind the gift. He was interested enough at last in Ponsonby to ask:

"How come you tangled with that rhino?"

"How did *I*—" Ponsonby was all injured innocence. "I wasn't doing a thing. 'Pon my word, I was just chugging peacefully along when suddenly the thing exploded out of the ground like a bally mine and came for me."

King nodded understanding.

"Yes, they look just like ant hills when they're lying down;

takes an experienced eye to spot 'em. And they'll charge anything that moves when they're mad, and this one's carrying
plenty of mad cause with him. I'd just about bet it was the same
one that winded my camp last night and hit it like a hurricane.
Among most everything else it stepped on my rifle." King's
wide mouth twisted. "Which is why you see me as helpless as
a toad."

"But if you need a rifle, I've got one in my car!"

"You got a—" King's whole expression altered, lifted out of
its dour dissatisfaction to the hope of a straitened swimmer
who sees the straw.

"Why, certainly, old fellow." Ponsonby's generous impulses
seemed to be without limit. "If you can use a rifle—Wait a sec.
I'll go get it."

Ponsonby returned from his car, beaming. He handed King
a shiny new weapon, the oil of its first packing not wiped from
it. "If you know how to use it, it's yours."

"Aa-ah!" King reached for it like a missionary for his bible.
He turned it over in his hands and drew the bolt. He end-for-
ended it and squinted through the barrel and—"Yes," he said.
"It *is* a rifle. But—" His white man inhibitions deterred him
from putting into words the Masai's outspoken comment about
the *panga* knife. He turned the sentence. "But, having even this,
when the rhino came for you, why the hell didn't you haul off
and stop it? The thing's one of your heavy British five-o-seven's.
You could at least have discouraged the brute."

"You mean—" Ponsonby stared at him, "You mean I should
have stopped my car and—" the thought was too bizarre for
words.

KING LAID the gun down. And Africa picked that
moment for another display of humor. The sun dipped to throw
long spiky shadows of the rocky outcrops that broke the plain;
and, as it might have been some intercepted ray device that
actuated machinery, a rumbling grumble reverberated in the
air. It had a peculiar quality of not loudness so much as an all

pervading volume that drummed in the ears. As it swelled, other rumbles took tip the signal from other rocky *kloofs* till the whole atmosphere vibrated to grumbling summer thunder out of which boomed the punctuations of coughing belly roars.

King was watching Ponsonby from under his lowered hat brim. He had watched all kinds of reactions to the first hearing of that African choir in an open auditorium. Ponsonby was watching King, absurdly quizzical with the monocular distortion of half his face. He said only.

"What do we do now?"

"What would you have done if you'd been in your car alone?"

"I'd have turned up the windows and sat tight." Ponsonby repeated it as a lesson. "They told me that lions didn't know enough to break in."

"There's a Hottentot proverb," said King. "The gods give either guts or sense."

"Meaning what?" Ponsonby was not attuned to native turns of thought.

"Meaning Englishmen." But King's interest in Ponsonby was now sufficient to ask: "Will you tell me what you're doing in this far end of nowhere without a keeper?"

Ponsonby was not offended. His indignation was directed, rather, at another cause. "Damn it, I tried to. I wanted to get a white hunter to guide me out, but d'you know what those brigands charge?"

King nodded. "A hundred pounds a month and expenses."

"Why, it's sheer banditry!"

King was not offended either. "Um-hm. But a white hunter often enough brings his babe out of the woods alive, and that's a chore that I know the worth of as well as anybody."

"You mean you're a white hunter?" Ponsonby was all eager excitement.

"Um-hm. There's been times when I've taken folks out—and brought 'em back."

"Why, then you could guide me to—" Ponsonby's eagerness chilled away to a blankness that dropped his monocle again.

"I say, old chap! No offense, you know. I mean, about fees and all that."

"No, no offense," said King. "I'm not hiring out anyway. I'm on my way into Entoto, nearest point where I can buy me a decent gun and be a man again, and nothing is stopping me. Only I'm more amazed about you than anything that's happened in a long while. It's none of my business, except that it's my business to understand the why of things in Africa. So will you tell me why? You're not hunting; you're not photographing. Is it maybe that you—but no; you're not writing. Will you tell me then why you want to be guided by the hand through the back reaches of Africa?"

Ponsonby's candor was quite un-British and engaging, but his explanation still made no better sense than any of the rest of him. "Well, you see, I was about to be dismissed from my job; so, since the emoluments were considerable, I had to put the old bean to work to find out why, and here I am."

"Just as simple as that." King remained patient. "You were going to get fired, judging by your complexion, out of a good job in England, so you came to Africa and got lost."

Ponsonby drew in a long breath of patience. "It's really all quite simple. I was—I still am, I suppose—export manager for a firm of steel manufacturers and our business has been falling off no end."

"So you came to the middle of Africa?"

"Yes, of course. To find out why these dashed trader blighters wouldn't carry our line of produce."

A wary, alert look like a leopard's came into King's eyes, but he grinned at the discomfiture he was about to produce.

"There's times, in between of guiding greenhorns, that I've been called all kinds of a Yankee trader myself."

"You are?" Ponsonby's eager enthusiasm suffused him again. "Why, then you're the very man I want to meet. You can—"

Surging realization loosened his monocle again to drop with his jaw. "I say, old man! Seems I put my foot into it every time."

King still grinned. "I'm not even trading. I'm on my way shortest cut to Entoto."

CHAPTER II

BLOOD DEBT

THE HOTTENTOT came and arranged sticks for the beginning of a fire. A short distance off the Masai was hacking at dry thorn scrub with the new *panga* and pausing at every few strokes to see whether its edge held. King gave the Hottentot camp instructions.

"A couple of fires will be enough for tonight. If Simba should come, I suppose this thing—" He pointed distastefully at the new rifle—"will suffice for close range." He added an explanation to Ponsonby. "No need for a thorn *boma* tonight, though this kind of rock outcrop country is a wasps' nest of 'em. But zebra and wildebeeste are plentiful and lions prefer them to us. Anything comes around tonight will be sheer damn cat curiosity, unless there's one of 'em mad about something."

"My word!" Ponsonby stared at him. "You fellows take them pretty casual."

King laughed at the incongruity. "Listen who's talking. You sell trade hardware, so you came out with a car, just like you'd take a turn of your midland towns in little old Blighty, to look over your territory in Africa?"

"Dash it all, man, I had to find out. The job's too good to lose."

"Whom d'you sell for?"

"Braun and Wendel. And all my samples and literature are in my car. So don't you see—" Ponsonby broke off at the sudden change in King's face. His jaw sagged as though the name had in some manner offered offense.

King's grin was taking its long time in contracting out of his lips, as a man who has been shot vitally may die with a death grin on his face. But King's eyes had already gone hard and had stared through Ponsonby and out into vistas that lay beyond the horizon of view. Ponsonby felt for his monocle, polished it without ever removing his transfixed gaze from King's, tried mechanically to twist it into his eye, from which, unsupported, it fell. He kept repeating the process while King still stared through him.

King's voice came at last; there was accusation in it.

"D'you know anything about steel?"

"Er, no," Ponsonby said. His voice had lost its buoyant enthusiasm. "No, I'm not a technician, just on the sales promotion end."

King grunted. "Well, then, let me tell you something about steel. I'm no technician either; I'm just a trader. But I'll tell you this—"

King, squatting there on a low rock, earth-stained, a little ragged, with the African dusk falling about him, loomed like some earnest exponent of a great religion delivering a world truth.

"Steel means *life!*"

The dictum delivered, he brooded over it, scowling into the gloom. Kaffa the Hottentot came and lit the camp-fire. Immediately the outer dusk that had merged tawny forms invisible into their background of tumbled boulders was punctuated by the reflections of great twin orbs that blinked and went out and opened to stare glassy green again. Kaffa shouted and threw burning sticks. The eyes blinked away and were silently gone.

King brooded on.

"In Africa, a man lives or dies by the quality of his steel."

King squatted silhouetted against the last copper glow of

the dusk. Ponsonby sensed, rather than saw, that his eyes were now boring into his own.

"That *panga* knife that you gave Barounggo. It was one of your samples?"

Ponsonby felt a certain guilt in admitting it.

King relapsed into his brooding, dark and pregnant of the things beyond Ponsonby's understanding. "Maybe," King rumbled, "I *am* just the man you need to meet. Maybe the gods of Africa have been manipulating the strings of fate." Suddenly he fired a lean, strong finger at Ponsonby like a gun. "Piet Vreeden carried your line, didn't he?"

Ponsonby had already been uneasy about a something not entirely satisfactory about Piet Vreeden. "Yes, he used to be one of my steadiest customers. They told me, as I came through, that he had been ripped up by a leopard."

"That was the report that came through to the district officials," King said grimly. "But I'll tell you this: Piet Vreeden was ripped open and his bowels festooned along a village fence by three men of the *Mathehebu wa Chui,* the leopard society!"

"Good Lord!" Ponsonby's stout British subservience to constituted law was outraged. "Didn't you inform the police?'"

"No." King said it with staggering simplicity. "Because two of those men had lost a brother and one a son who died because the steel spear blades that Vreeden had traded them failed them when their need came."

"Good Lord!"

KING TWISTED on his rock to point into the sky glow that smoldered its last dull anger. "Right there. Right back in that country from where I was coming and you were heading when we met." He relapsed to his rumination again; out of which came the growling conviction growling: "Yeah. Maybe I'm the white hunter you need to guide you by the hand and show you things that a lot of smug money-makers in England ought to know."

His voice was hard and practical. "I was headed for Entoto

*Then he saw the rhino,
appallingly close.*

and I bragged that nothing would stop me. But I don't buck the gods of Africa. If they sent you I'll take you. To your own territory, that you wanted to look over and learn why." He called to the dark shapes of his two henchmen who huddled over the very smoke of their fire as only Africans can. "Tomorrow we trek back and go into the country of the Watanga tribes."

"*Ow, Bwana!*" The querulous complaint came from Kaffa the Hottentot. "An evil people and hostile to white man. Moreover it is a country unknown to us and the report was that trade amongst them was difficult."

King grinned at Ponsonby. "Difficult. But I'll take you in and show you your territory, by golly. Even with no better a gun than this one to make a man of me."

Ponsonby fidgeted on his rock seat, Britishly abashed over the necessary intrusion of finance. "Awf'ly good of you and all that. But, er—I'm afraid I can't quite afford to pay that frightful white hunter fee, you know."

"You aren't hiring me." King's voice was as hot as the glow in his eyes. "This is a call, a mission put on me by the gods of Africa."

It was only his laugh, a little ribald, that saved him from melodrama. "Anyway, I was figuring to edge in on that Watanga country some day and get acquainted, maybe scoop some of the business that Vreeden lost. I got a wagon load of trade at my friend Chief Muthengi's *boma*, waiting only till the Watanga might have forgotten some of their lousy deal."

A sudden thought came to cloud King's decisions. He fired his finger at Ponsonby again. "If, that is to say, you've got the guts to go through a piece of territory spoiled by your man."

Ponsonby's monocle dropped while he stared. He said querulously: "Well, dash it all, I came to find out, didn't I?"

King's appraisal of Ponsonby showed itself in a sour scrutiny that slowly broke into a grin.

"The rest of the Hottentot proverb," he said, "is that sense, if the little gods have withheld it, can be added to guts by the great god of Experience. I'll maybe even bring you out of the woods alive. Which, if I do, you'll be useful."

"I rather think, old chap," Ponsonby said, "you're trying to spoof me. You don't look at all nervous about it yourself."

King's sardonic grin slowly hardened.

"In Africa—" He told Ponsonby the priceless rule—"a back country trader keeps alive by not letting the native know that he's nervous. Only he's got to be careful. A white man, armed, can get through a lot of Africa these days, if he doesn't let himself get caught napping, like Vreeden. He relied on his native woman to tip him off to anything cooking up against him; his trouble was she happened to be related to one of the men who died. No, sir—there's a lot of people in this land have said I'm no good, but they'll all admit I'm damned careful."

THE WAGON lurched in vast drunken progress over the uneven plain; square-hooded like a truck, its wheels as high as a man's shoulder, they heaved slowly up over grass tussocks and ant bear mounds that the most skilled guiding could not avoid, and they came down on the other side with a crash that wrenched at every joint. It took eight span of cattle to haul the ponderous thing—sixteen oxen and two black boys who cracked twenty-foot whips about their ears and yelled with vast African exuberance.

There was never any secret about a trade wagon coming into a country. This one's progress served hardy notice that King came not as an official, not as a missionary, nor as a hunter, but out and out as a trader and nothing else.

It was a country of umbrella-topped acacias and great brown termite hills that looked like clustered roofs of huts.

"Poor agricultural country," King commented.

Ponsonby trudged beside him, interested but not impressed.

King expounded, "If you're interested in ethnology—which a trader should be and Piet Vreeden was not—this crowd hasn't evolved to an agricultural civilization; they're cattle raisers, therefore nomads who follow the grass, therefore a tougher crowd than the farmers we left in Muthengi's country."

"Do you mean, difficult to trade with?"

"To get along with."

"Why?"

"For one reason, they've got little to lose in a fight. Their property is on the hoof: they can run it into the brush. For another thing, being loose on the hoof, they've got to be ready to defend it against man or beast, and where there's fat cattle there's fatter lions and leopards and things. Hell, it's history. Masai, Gauchos, cow punchers, they've all got to be fighting men."

Ponsonby digested that over a plodding half mile. Then, "Would you tell me, old chap, why you're doing this?"

King laughed harshly. "Because I'm a trader. Because I want to crash this territory before some one else gets ahead of me."

Then Ponsonby said. "I rather fancy, old man, you're spoofing me again."

"Yeah?"

"Yes, I have an idea, don't you know, that you're a sort of a Quixote chappie who believes that good fighting men, whatever their color, ought to have good weapons to fight with."

"Boloney!" King said.

Ponsonby laughed at him.

"You gave me credit once for perception," he said.

The wagon creaked and crashed for three days through that country before the brown ant hills in the distance turned out at last to be a village.

"We'll have to trade for meat," King said. "Where cattle eat off the grazing there's been no game. Watch now; you'll learn something."

The village was a filth-littered alley between flimsy huts of bare poles that could be left without loss when the middens became too pestilential for even African nostrils and the populace moved away to better pastures.

King stopped before the fence that surrounded the largest hut. He refrained from the white man blunder of barging in. Through the interlaced branches of the fence could be seen women and goats and lounging men. None came forward with the big toothed grin and the "*Jambo, Bwana,*" of greeting that had met them at Muthengi's boma. King nodded to Baroung-go.

The Masai planted the steel spike of his spear butt in the ground between the gate poles; the slender, three-foot blade of it quivered its tempered steel in the sun. As a Masai he knew how to speak to lesser peoples, as he knew that they knew a Masai's worth.

"Out!" he shouted. "Out, little head man and be humble when the *Bwana,* master of an Elmoran, waits."

There was some scuffling and much muttering within the hut and through its interstices it could be seen that a man was dressing himself; that is to say, he was draping a sheet, rendered impervious to rain by boiling in rancid butter, about his shoulders. Respectfully dressed but sullen, he came to his gateway and stood on one leg, the heel of the other cupped in the hollow of his knee, leaning against a spear for balance.

"*Jambo,* Masai," he said. He kept his eyes averted from the necessity of greeting the white men.

"We require," Barounggo ordered him, "six fat goats, or a young calf. We give one spear in exchange."

Other men came to balance themselves at their gates; tall naked fellows, they said nothing but looked on in lowering silence, while the head man was telling the Masai with barefaced effrontery, "We have no fat goats."

"A spear head," King told Ponsonby, "is damned good payment for half a dozen goats."

"Lie not!" The Masai growled at the head man. "Do I not see a good fat goat there?"

An obvious lie in Africa is only a form of expression. The man laughed insolently. "Let me then see your good spear head."

THE MASAI folded his great arms. Bargaining was no thing for an Elmoran. It was the little Hottentot, keen as an ape to prove his wits in a trade, who hopped forward with a blade.

The head man fingered it, turned it around in his hands. Others of the men unhinged their legs and came forward. A spear trade was as important as a deal in a new automobile.

King nudged Ponsonby. "Look at the big buck with the scars."

The man he indicated was gashed with four parallel scars that spanned forehead, cheek, and chin from nose to ear.

"Leopard society mark. Tell you about it later. Watch the

trade now for your soul's good. I don't like the looks of this set-up."

The men handled the blade, smelled at it, whittled a stick with it. Their faces remained dubious.

"There's a slogan you birds have," King told Ponsonby grimly: "British steel. There's places around the world where its a proud slogan. This is not one of them. And the hell of it is there's more places than this in Africa where it isn't, like some of your sleek business barons will be learning some day."

Ponsonby said nothing. But his face was flushed.

"Look at 'em," King told him. "Look at 'em well. There's one sample of why your gang's business is falling off. These dumb oxen can't read brand marks stamped into the article; they won't know whether a spear blade is any good till they've had to use it—and then it's maybe too late for anything but collecting the blood price off the trader. There's times the price can be settled with gifts to the family; but blood debts can stack up till there's no price but blood. These surly fellows haven't forgotten your Vreeden— All right, Kaffa, take the five goats that they offer and let's get going."

The wagon creaked and crashed on its way. There were no shouts of, "*Kua heri,* or "*Ya-kuonana,*" meaning "May we meet again;" no women jostling to wheedle a safety pin or a key ring to hang into their ear lobes.

"An insolent village." The Masai growled as he stalked.

"An ill village to trade and hostile, as I warned *Bwana* before ever we came," the Hottentot complained.

"A leopard village," King told Ponsonby. "That fellow thought he was big and tough enough not to take orders, so the Mahethebu wa Chui marked him."

For all of King's studied casualness, Ponsonby felt the chill tingle of one of Africa's darker aspects.

"What about these leopards, old man? Doesn't the Colonial government do anything about them?"

King shrugged. "They keep trying. But it's a big job and it

covers a lot of terri-
tory. The Maheth-
ebu is as secret as
the Mafia. They
meet masked, a sort
of vigilante society
or a Ku-Klux with
African trimmings.
Anybody doesn't do
what he's told, they
jump him some
night and put the
four gash marks on
him with steel claws
on their fingers.
Anybody they've
really got it in for,
they pin him
spread-eagled up

*"Watch out! Now is the time
to show them death!"*

against the village fence with a big wooden skewer through
each upper arm and disembowel him with one swipe. Colonial
police can never find out anything 'cause nobody dares to
squeal."

Like all nomadic people, the Watanga lived in patriarchal,
or clan, groups; each clan claimed grazing rights over certain
territory and each carried its own distinguishing marks.

It was in the next clan territory that the distinguishing mark
obtruded itself with an unpleasant jolt. The business of trading
for food was accomplished by the same sulks that left King
hardily unperturbed, but it was while a tall warrior was showing
his sullen suspicion of the hardware offered that King felt the
back of his head being positively bored into by Kaffa's eyes.

"Keep an eye peeled," he told Ponsonby. "The Hottentot has
something." He knew that the little man's eyes missed less than
would any monkey and he turned with casual assurance of ease.

"Aa-ah!" King's exhalation drew Ponsonby's head around in a flash. "Look at that guy's spear. Notice anything?"

"No—oh yes, these fellows spear heads are little short ones, not like your big chap's young sword."

"I mean, about their ornamentation around the haft?"

"No."

"Well." A brittleness was in King's voice. "It's the same as the broken end that stuck in your rhino."

"Was there a broken—I never noticed a—" Ponsonby's monocle fell to dangle on its string. "Good Lord, d'you mean to say that—"

His stare had the taut strain of a dawning nausea.

KING'S ATTITUDE of calm assurance had slipped from him like an unwanted cloak. His whole body tightened up to wary expectation of the anything that could happen in Africa. His eyes, pinched narrow, were flitting to light momentarily on every detail of the scene—the groupings of tall sullen men, their attitudes, the expressions on their individual faces, he noted each and flashed to the next. He spoke without looking at Ponsonby.

"Means nothing—yet. Could be no more than just cussed coincidence. A spear could be traded from hand to hand across the continent. Or a nomadic hunter might travel a hundred miles. Or, at its worst, it could have happened right here, and a molested animal will then often travel a hundred miles, and a hundred is just about what we've come—Come along, Kaffa. Close the deal and let's move on into the open."

He said it in English. The little Hottentot would never admit that he could understand a word. But the deal was closed; the whip boys yelled and crackled little puffs of dust about their catties' ears; the wagon lurched and creaked on its protesting way.

King let it pass and fell in behind its dust, a rear guard against he didn't know what, stiff and erect, his back broad to whatever might be behind.

"Don't look back," he told Ponsonby. "Never let man or meat-eating beast smell a sign of nervousness." Out of the side of one eye he watched Ponsonby square his shoulders and adjust his monocle with a flourish. A laugh was always a good offset to any taint of nervousness. So King contrived one for the scowling populace.

"If your back crawls like mine, Britisher," he crackled his parting laugh, "we'll need a drink when we get out of this."

At the end of the village the drivers' sudden onslaught on their beasts swerved the wagon to scrape the very wall of the last hut. The Hottentot, too, stood to let it pass and fell in behind King to mutter:

"The middle of the road, *Bwana!* The wheels have not touched it."

King saw and stepped over it without changing his stride. It was a design marked on the ground so recently that tiny scrapings of earth still fell into the depressions; a rough oblong, each side of it consisted of four parallel lines scored deep in the hard packed dirt. Twigs and beans, prettily spotted, marked a design within the design.

"Bad medicine," King muttered, and he swore emphasis to it. "Damned bad medicine."

Well away from the village and out of sight behind mimosa scrub he called a halt.

"Council of war."

Ponsonby's innate sense of the proprieties were still unattuned to outlandish ideas.

"With your African servants?"

King grinned a rebuke. "Never having been a big shot office executive or an officer in an army, I got a crazy theory it's a square deal to the rank and file to let 'em talk their way out of the hole we're all of us in."

CHAPTER III

THE LEOPARDS' PREY

KAFFA THE Hottentot did most of the talking. Not an item had his eyes missed. "It was undoubtedly a *thahu*, *Bwana*, a curse laid in our path by a *mudu-mugu* of the leopards."

"The leopards, certainly," King agreed. "For the lines are the four claws, raked into the earth with steel. But we were not there very long; how do we know that a curse was built so swiftly for us? Could it not be just a sign that the village is one controlled by the Wa-Chui?"

The Hottentot's wizened face contorted into myriad wrinkles of astute delight in interpreting even bad luck. "But it is simple, *Bwana*. The long figure of four sides is no man's house, for houses are round. It is the wagon. The twigs were the *murumb-iru* shrub of sorcery and they were six, as we are six. The spotted beans of the castor oil were sixteen, as our cattle are sixteen and spotted."

"Damn if I don't believe you're right." King's frown studied the picture. "I don't suppose you could read just what the curse said?"

"Nay, *Bwana*, that is known only to the sorcerer who built the curse. We know only that the leopards are here and that they are hostile."

"And if they've got the gall to put the mark on a white man caravan, it means they're mad enough for mischief." King scowled into the distance from where they had come; then his brows lifted to shrug a dour optimism. "Maybe it's no more than a Ku Klux warning to stay the hell out of there. But all the same it'll be wise to be careful—and the best way to be careful, Little Wise Ape, is to up and run like devils other than the Wa-Chui were after us. Is it not so?"

The Masai growled his characteristic objection. "How many are we? Five good men; and even the white man with one good eye has courage and might be taught some small use. How many of the leopards can there be in one small village? Ten, perchance, or twenty? *Kefule!* Let us go back and demand an apology for this insolent witch writing."

The two whip boys only stared like their own oxen, round-eyed, willing to be led. The Hottentot chittered rage at the Masai. "So snorts *kifaru,* who has bulk but no wit. Children at monkey height know that where the leopards are strong they can order a whole tribe to sharpen their spears and blow the war horns. We know that they have been strong enough to tear the bowels from one trader because of his faithless metal. How will they know what trader's metal it was that betrayed their hunter to *kifaru? Bwana,* it is wiser that we go swiftly."

King nodded slowly, frowning down at his boot toe, and then more decidedly.

"Particularly, *Bwana,*" the Hottentot added a grim observation to clinch the argument, "since two of those *murumbiru* twigs, the two largest, were peeled with a knife, white around the middle."

"The hell you say!" King relieved Ponsonby's impatience with a translation of the discussion. "And two of the sticks represent particularly us with our bellies laid bare to the ill wind that blows. So we're going to shove our pride in our pockets and run like hell."

Ponsonby's eyes, as the full significance of it soaked in, began to widen. King watched for the monocle to drop. "D'you mean to say, old man—" It dropped. "Excuse the personality, my dear fellow, but if you propose to run, the situation must be pretty dashed serious, eh? You mean you're going to abandon the wagon and all that and leg it?"

"Damned if I will." King bit on the obstinate refusal. "Let 'em know they've got us scared, and the whole district will be up and whooping on our trail. We're still armed white men—or at any rate one of us. We can hold 'em off in open country. But it's wiser to get out of this district instead of bulling on through. These people are more on the prod than I figured, what with this rhino trouble and all. We'll just head out southeast for the M'tusi country. That's traded by a fellow I know, and he carried a decent line of goods."

So southeast the wagon lumbered its labored course, steering wide of distant clustered ant hills that might turn out to be villages.

But dim drums throbbed in the hot air behind them and other drums whispered gutturally back from in front of them.

"I don't like it," King growled. "Drums could be no more than native jamboree, but they could be anything else, and these rhythms are new even to Kaffa." Savagely he rubbed in the lesson. "Here's one example of what lousy trade goods can do."

Ponsonby produced the standard defense.

"But it's an accepted business principle, my dear fellow. Export goods, so long as they're better than the local supply, always find a market. For African savages, then—what I mean, people practically in the stone age, any sort of a—"

King wouldn't let him finish. "That's a matter that'll boomerang back on your fat manufacturers one of these fine days. Nor I don't give a hoot if its cheap perfumery or shoddy cotton goods and tin pots. Any smart white man can come back and argue himself a repeat order on a worn out gee string. But weapons—steel—that's something else again."

"I'm beginning to see—"

"Damned right you are. Savages are practical people; their reasoning goes no farther than cause and direct effect. Lousy weapons, death, blood price. That's one cash consideration for your businessmen to look at, even if they don't give a hoot about somebody else's life."

His growl coughed harshly from him like a charging lion's.

"So here's us; two white men getting chased out of a district that's in a British colony—*If* we get out. I can't read those drums but, by golly, I know a war horn when I hear one. *Eweh,* there! You cattle drivers! Head for that rock *kloof.* We'll hole up till we see what's what."

BY THE time they gained the rock outcrop and King, ferociously swearing, had found defensive shelter between boulders that suited him, the drumming that had been pervading the horizon had come to a focus. It was hidden, still, behind mimosa scrub, but every now and then a wave of yells rose out of the muttering roll.

"Talking up their courage," King grunted. "A mob is a mob wherever you find it. My guess is that our friends the leopards are whooping up the populace for a lynching." He slammed open the bolt of Ponsonby's new rifle, scowled disgustedly into the mechanism; then he broke open several packets of cartridges and laid them in fives, ready to hand.

Ponsonby watched him with the fascination of unbelief in what he saw.

"But, my dear fellow, this is a British colony! Pacified years ago and policed by rural constabulary, so they told me. There can't be a bally open war like this."

"Sure a British colony." King kicked rubble from under his shooting position. "A district official comes on tour every six months and collects hut tax and a white policeman rides through it every now and then and the local headmen come to his tent and report all quiet on the Western front. Sure it's pacified. And when this is all over, whichever way it goes, it'll still be all quiet. Because the officials will never hear a peep about any of it, unless it'll be that two more white men had an unfortunate accident with a leopard, or got bit by a snake or something. A lot of things can happen to a man in Africa. The Wa-Chui, I'm telling you, are more secret than the Mafia. It's black men keeping a secret against white. Certainly this country is pacified."

By this time the mob had come into sight. Dark shapes

detached themselves from the farther tree boles and massed in a hesitant horde on the plain below.

"Humh! A good hundred of 'em. Well, a good white man with white man weapons has held off more than that of savages before now. Barounggo, go on down and tell 'em to get the hell back to their homes before widows will be tearing the spirit hole in the thatch."

"My sacred word!" King was becoming more unbelievable to Ponsonby by the minute. "You take it jolly cool."

King was able to grin at him under his frown of preoccupation. "Excitement neither thinks nor shoots straight. What's more, it takes disciplined men and leadership to rush a position against accurate rifle fire, and your Pax Britannica has taught the colored brother all about white man superiority. Taught 'em a long range rifle is better than a whole lot of spears."

Barounggo was striking his arrogant posture before the crowd. Naked except for a serval cat skin girdle, the wind ruffled his black ostrich plumes and monkey tail garters, the sun threw his great muscles up in high lights of yellow brown, glinted a long sharp line from his spear. A menacing figure, he swaggered before the mob. Imperious, belligerent, he shouted commands at them. They lowered before him like oxen. But here and there out of the crowd voices shouted back. The distance was a good three hundred yards, to far to distinguish what was being said.

King grunted. "See those conical hoods of straw bobbing about amongst them? And you'll note they keep well in the rear. Leopard men, masked, whooping 'em on."

"I thought there'd be more." King's coolness was vastly reassuring to Ponsonby. "I only see about ten."

"It's enough." King barked a sardonic laugh. "It's the same in any color; the lads smart enough to organize an ogpu talk the dumb clucks into doing the storm troop stuff. Damn, with a gun of my own I could pick some of those coyotes off from right here. But—" His mouth twisted down at the rifle.

Barounggo was stalking back. Before reporting to King he

stood on a rock and waved his spear above his head in a wide threatening circle. Then he stood before his white master.

"They are insolent cattle, *Bwana,* and their talk has the cunning of leopards but the honor of hyaenas that eat corpses. They say, *Bwana,* that they have no war with black men, who are all dupes together. But the two white traders, they say, must pay the price of blood with blood. Therefore, if we black men agree, we may leave you here and walk away in peace. But if we do not agree, then I must wave my spear around as a signal and who falls in the fight, it is his fate."

"I take it," King said dryly, "that you decided for all of you."

"Nay, *Bwana.*" The great fellow laughed his arrogant assurance. "What choice was there in such a decision? Can a man bargain with hyaenas?"

King stood up from his crouched position and reached a hand to grip the Masai's muscled shoulder. The rough tremor that went through his arm was all that he said. But his short laugh joined Barounggo's and his surge of pride was not above telling the thing to Ponsonby.

"Dashed sporting, I call it," said Ponsonby. "I jolly well knew he was a gentleman."

The creases of King's short humor about his mouth merged into other creases, deep set, very hard. His eyes pinched down to far sighting narrowness.

"So now they'll be coming." He crouched down to shooting position again. "I hate to do this," he growled. "These bullets will knock a hole in a man as big as a plate. And you can bet those masked Chui coyotes will see to it that it won't be their fate to get hit."

"*Ngalio, Bwana!*" The Hottentot shrilled warning. "Watch out! Now is the time to show them! That tall fellow, *Bwana,* who leaps high there towards the left. See, he leads a group of his household."

"Ye-eh! Poor dumb devil! He's got to be stopped." The heavy rifle roared out. The wretched man spun as though he had been hit with a sledge hammer and sprawled to be hidden in the grass. His yelling, eager troop shrank back into the mob.

THE MOB milled and howled. The sun on brandished spear heads twinkled like stars over a black night. Voices shrilled above the mob's hoarse hubbub; they were the standard tones of the Wa-Chui designed to copy the snarl of a leopard and to disguise their voices.

"Lousy balance," King grated. "The thing kicks like an old eight gauge, and throws high to left. That man should have dropped flat."

"Another one, *Bwana!* To the right of middle there! He with the ochred hair eggs on his troop."

The Masai stood impassively aloof and watched lesser men die. He took a little horn from his ear lobe, tapped snuff from it onto his great blade and sniffed it up with a windy inhalation.

The oxen drivers squatted and stared with white rolling eyes.

Ponsonby took out his monocle, polished it, put it back, took it out, polished it.

"Good Lord!" he kept repeating, and, "My sacred aunt!"

"To the left again, *Bwana!*" The Hottentot shrilled.

That overzealous leader paid his price.

"I say, old man!" Ponsonby was awed, his ruddy face white. "This is a pretty ghastly lesson, what?"

"To them?" King flared again as he spoke.

"To me. I mean about—well, trade goods and Africans and all that sort of thing."

"Told you you'd"—King fired again—"you'd learn. Experience is—Hell, they're coming fast!"

He snatched a five of cartridges, juggled them into the breech, fired, slammed out the bolt, fired. "Got to stop that rush, by—God!" The cry tore from King's throat as might a man's last strong cry in life.

"The blasted thing's jammed!"

He wrenched out his hunting knife and pried at the bolt in a frenzy. Then his breath fought strangled from him like a death rattle.

"No it isn't. It's broken!"

His hands on the gun gripped it as though they would in sheer agony of frustration twist the useless thing to further fragment. His throat gulped at its constriction and let his voice through, dry and flat, like somebody else quoting a platitude.

"Steel!" it said. "Cheap steel!"

The Masai bounded out of his impassivity. The Hottentot was already pawing at the weapon in King's hands.

"What goes wrong, *Bwana?* What so great evil is in *Bwana's* voice?"

It was not by any stretch of reflection Ponsonby's direct fault. But King looked only at him. He answered the question to him.

"White men," he said. "Weaponless!"

The mob below had been stopped by the grisly effect of those deadly smashing bullets. But only a few seconds of hesitant milling showed them that no more came. Their half-cowed shouting swelled to encouraging yells, surged to a roar of howling. Shrill leopard voices squealed high behind them. Their rush came in a dark stampede of straining bodies and twinkling spears.

Barounggo bounded to the front and stood on wide planted feet, his spear couched in both hands. His deep laugh rolled from him in a continuous growl.

King screamed at him. "No use, Barounggo! Drop it! Drop it, you damned fool!"

Barounggo never looked back.

"Some will yet eat spear. *Ss-ssghee!*" he shouted. "Come, cattle herders. An Elmoran of the Masai waits."

THERE WAS never any impractical heroism about King. His belief that anything could happen in Africa was supported by a sturdy conviction that, according to all the laws of chance, the happening could just as well be good, and if it was not, then an alert opportunist might yet turn bad to good.

He rushed at the superb Masai maniac, took him unexpectedly. He snatched the great spear from him and flung it far behind. He screamed at him, "Six against a hundred! We give in. And if we white men survive the first spears there may yet be a chance."

He leaped back and scrambled to a high rock.

"Up!" he yelled to Ponsonby. "Up out of the first rush and let the leopards talk! They're not blood mad—not yet!"

High above the wave that surged up the incline, he held the rifle where everybody could see it and threw it away from him. The wave broke around the base of the rock, roaring. Spears thrust up at them. Screaming men jumped high to reach at them.

Leopard voices squealed high in command. The straw masks, like little steeples, fought to shove through to the now harmless front. Till presently there was a ring of them round the base of the rock, squealing and snarling for order.

Reluctantly the madness passed from the mob. Masks turned to stare at the most rebellious voices. The men cowered away from them.

A voice squeaked, "It is the white men. The white traders we take with us. Against black brothers we have no blood debt."

King looked down on it all. As ill a situation as the grim gods of Africa had ever shown him. He shrugged acceptance of he did not know what in store. His voice was flat and as grim as the turn that the gods had played on him.

He looked down at the Mahethebu-Wa-Chui. "The white men come. But our black servants go free."

A voice squeaked a shrill laugh from within a mask.

"The black men go free," it said.

"Come along," King told Ponsonby, "and hold a tight check on any superior ideas you may have about being manhandled by black men. Stand for anything, or the only argument you'll get will be a spear."

He slid down from the rock. Only two little pulsating ridges that swelled over his jaw muscles showed that he bit his teeth tight over whatever was to come. In silence as impassive as the Masai's he suffered the indignity of having his hunting knife wrenched from his belt, having himself pawed around, his hands tied behind him with grass rope.

It was the Masai who shouted, raved from beyond a barrier of a score of men who held spears to his chest. They laid insult on the Bwana Kingi, he roared. Kingi, *mwinda na simba,* the hunter of lions, *na pigana n'gagi na mikonake,* who fights gorillas with his hands. Kingi, whom an Elmoran is proud to serve. He shouted threats. He would make a war, he promised; he would raise twenty men and bring desolation to this insolent tribe.

He even demeaned himself to threaten that he would so far let vengeance out of his own hands as to bring the *Serkali,* the white man's government, down on this district.

Some of the spearmen turned away their faces so that they might not later be recognized. Some dropped their eyes and muttered half apologetically that they had no quarrel with the

Masai people; it was only white traders that they had been ordered to attack.

But a derisive voice squeaked out of a mask: "One white trader has paid a little of the overdue price for our many young men who have died. What difference is there in these two?"

"What difference?" King barked a bitter little laugh. "How can these people know the difference till they've tested the goods? All right, Barounggo. It's no use. Take charge of the wagon and take it out by way of the Ndolia mission. It is an order. I will meet you there. It is a promise."

Round holes turned to stare at the effrontery of it. No derisive comment came from any mask. Dully suspicious, the very attitudes of the grotesque little steeples of plaited straw, some thrust forward, some perked sideways, indicated that they wondered what unknown power this white man might still have up his sleeve that let him be so calm. But since no further portent emerged, no sudden modern magic of destruction, they gathered up their resolution and herded their prisoners before them. The rabble streamed down the hill to the open plain.

King growled a certain satisfaction. "That'll keep Baroung-go out of anything rash for a time, anyhow." He nudged Ponsonby with his elbow. "Go on, talk. Laugh. Make a show of it. The tougher we brag to these fellows, the more they'll think before doing anything."

Ponsonby's stiff British upper lip was able to respond. His tone remained as naturally casual as ever, even hopeful.

"Did you mean that, old man? About meeting your wagon at some mission? It wasn't just a—a Yankee bluff?"

King produced his hardy laugh. "Hell, the wagon's safer'n we are. Men can have an unfortunate accident and a village headman can offer the next constable patrol the evidence of bones that tell no tales. But goods talk. If any native village would suddenly be unduly rich in hardware, some bright policeman would start putting things together."

"Awf'y consoling and all that, my dear fellow, to know that

your wagon load of goods has a chance of getting out. Quite jolly. Ha-ha-ha—Haa-aah— Oh! Dammitall, there goes my bally eyeglass!"

It seemed so ludicrous that the monocle dangling on its string was the major tragedy that King cackled a response. The natives stared owl-eyed and muttered to one another over these white men who in their circumstances could still laugh.

THE CORTEGE reached the fringe of brush out of which it had come. The straw masks squeaked commands. The rank and file obediently drifted away in their various directions to their respective villages.

Only masks remained to prod their prisoners with spears into a path that none of the others followed.

King grunted. "So the Leopard Society stages a private performance before it gets to the dirty work along the village thorn fence. That's something I didn't know about them."

Ponsonby stared at him with eyes as blank as holes in a mask. "Seems to me these chappies—nine or ten of them, aren't there?—would be enough to do something pretty ghastly to just two of us with our hands tied."

King grated a harsh chuckle. "That order about taking care of the wagon wasn't all of it a bluff. It kept the boys out of any foolhardy trouble when blood ran hot and it leaves us now with four men free and wide open to help us. Four good men to ten or eleven is a heap better odds than to a hundred."

Ponsonby remained pessimistic. And reasonably so. Hands tied, hustled by spear points that callously drew blood with every prod, driven like a sacrificial goat along a faint trail that twisted through thick thorn scrub, he was hardly to be blamed.

"Four African servants." He stated his near despair, and his smile was only a set grimace now.

"Not servants," King snapped. "Two of them, perhaps, the two drivers. But the other two are men who've been through enough tough spots with me to stand by in this one."

"Your Masai, yes," Ponsonby conceded gloomily. "But how

long will it take him to round up any help? How long have we got before—" He wet his lips to continue the grisly thought that was in his mind, and then shut them down tight on it.

"Not the Masai. Kaffa."

"The little Hottentot? Why, he's the timid one!"

King scowled his troubled introspection as he plodded along. At times his lips tightened over his memories; at times they let go again to break in the beginnings of a pale smile. "Timid—like an ape. He can't offer to fight the world single-handed, yet I've seen a hamadryas baboon jump a leopard when his superior intelligence told him his chance was good. It's wits we'll need to get us out of this hole, if at all. And wits is what the little Hottentot fights with."

"I hope you're jolly well right, old man. The nearer that sun gets toward night, the less I can keep from thinking of Piet Vreeden. And listen to these fellows. They're talking in their normal voices now. Seem pretty cold sure that nobody will be in a position to give evidence against them. D'you want me to laugh just to show my bally nerve?"

King did not ask him to laugh. He did not laugh himself. He said only: "This much at least we're sure of: they're not warriors and they're a secret organization, just smart enough to get braver men to do the front line fighting for them—and there's folks who hold that a gang that operates under masks isn't so long on guts."

It was little enough comfort.

It was still daylight when the twisty path suddenly turned another corner and came out on a clearing in the thorn scrub. Not a village, just a space that stank of human usage and had a fringe of huts around a third or so of its arc. A little apart was a single, much larger hut. That was all. That and the close, thorn jungle.

The white men were shoved into a hut, darkly odorous. Nobody said anything to them. But two broad spear heads that moved in silhouette before the open oblong of the doorway showed that escape would be a futile thought. Not a sound came from outside; there was only the blank silence of the jungle in that period before the dusk when the day creatures are thinking of sleep and the night creatures are thinking of waking up.

Through the doorway the prisoners could see the solitary larger hut, over its doorway the ominous fraternity insignia. A white leopard skull.

"Pretty slick," King grunted. "If any copper should ever chance on this, all they'd have to do would be to hide away that skull and the place would be an innocent *thiringa,* a community club house for the unmarried men who get troublesome around the village women and so get chased out by the elders."

"Really, old fellow," Ponsonby snapped at him. "I can't get interested in African ethnology just now. How are your wrists? Any chance of wriggling free?" His own dry panting showed that he strained at his own ropes.

He fell silent. There was nothing cheerful to talk about.

CHAPTER IV

DANCE OF DEATH

DARKNESS CAME. The night woke up and talked the dark secrets of the jungle in its varied tongues— trills, squeals, snarls. No honest, full throated lion voices, for the jungle holds none. All the voices were furtive, all engaged in the merciless necessity of killing some smaller thing to eat. The moon came up to let shadows crawl over the yellow ground. The broad spear heads moved restlessly before the doorway.

It was Ponsonby who suddenly uttered a gasping, "Good God!"

"Huh?" King had been brooding over his slender hopes, his eyes focussed on nothing.

"An—er, a large animal just ran out of the jungle. Right into the door of the big hut. It—I thought it looked like a leopard!"

"Aa-ah!" King's throat made the form of his characteristic exclamation, but the sound of it was nearer to a moan than he cared to let himself hear. He swallowed hard before he was able to say, "I've heard of this. *M'cheso mya Chui,* the leopard dance."

"What does it mean—for us?"

"Not so good." King held his voice hard between his teeth. "A sort of cat and mouse game with their victims. Keeps the mice just alive till the cats get tired and take 'em over to the village thorn fence to let the public see what happens."

Ponsonby said nothing. King heard him swallow dryly in the dark. The "animal" came out of the big hut. First a flat head with wide gaping teeth, white in the moonlight; it peered with feline caution round the doorway. Then the spotted body followed, sinuously hugging the door post. It crouched. Then it emitted a throaty, mm'mr-r-r-row, like a magnified cat calling to its family and it rolled in a moon patch to bat at the air.

Then Ponsonby could see the spotted legs flat and tied over the man's chest and flanks. Another leopard ambled towards it, out of one of the smaller huts. The first one, with marvelous agility, leaped high and away and poised with arched back.

Others came to join in the dance—the play, rather, as each of them had watched leopards play in the jungle and now copied their gambols. The human rendition of it forcefully emphasized that the whole play of the great cats is designed by Nature for practise for the two sole purposes of their lives; either for the capture and cruel wearing down of their prey, or for fighting amongst the males, the tactics of which is to grapple and disembowel the antagonist.

King whispered, "When they get tired of that, they'll pull us out. Leaving our legs free so we can run like rats and make sport."

Ponsonby was able to keep a steady voice. "Looks like a sticky end, old man, D'you suppose, if we could kick one of them good and hard in the right places, he'd get savage enough to make it quick?"

But the leopard men were not tiring of their play yet. They seemed to possess all the vitality of the cats they copied. The moon was coming up behind the prison hut. As though by calculated refinement of cruel design, the black door framed the shapes of the broad guarding spears and the moon-flecked jungle amphitheater with its back drop of the leopard house.

It was a consummate imitation that the fraternity brothers, with all their savage faculty for mimicry, gave of feline play. Purring against the door posts like homing cats, sniffing the air for danger; madly across the clearing, frisking in the jungle fringe.

Something he had never noticed before was forced on Ponsonby's half hypnotized fascination—that the cats are noisy only in actual fight.

In the broken light it was startlingly easy to take them for the beasts they copied, but the moon glinted silver every now and then from great steel claws.

Only the muted pad of feet and the furry chafe of colliding bodies came. The surrounding jungle shuffled and squeaked and furtively crouched to watch man, the master beast, prance.

It was King whose sudden shout showed how tautly the spectacle had been stretching his nerves.

Immediately a leopard-capped head peered inside. The rest of the body followed and the rank stench of ill cured hide filled the hut as the wearer groped to assure himself that the prisoners remained tied.

The man grunted assurance to his companion and went out.

King's whisper to Ponsonby was fierce in its exultation. "By God, I knew he'd figure out something! Watch that leopard by the jungle's edge! Just around that big tree trunk! That littlest leopard of the lot!"

The smallest leopard emerged to prance with the others.

"D'you mean—?" The question was hoarse in Ponsonby's throat.

"Cripes a'mighty, I told you he was smart. Watch him imitate the others. Timid, huh? Like an ape."

The little leopard's mimicry was exquisite. He cat-footed with the others. He rolled on his back and batted at moon shadows; he let himself be chased and sprang away sideways on stiff legs. He chased others. He hid as they hid—

And carefully he pranced always in the most shadowy spots.

The clearing would be empty for long pauses at a time, filled only with a sense of intent watching from behind obstacles; the emptiness broken by a rush of bodies that would almost meet headlong, would leap high and would race away to be chased into hiding again.

The smallest leopard leaped with them, raced from them, sat on his haunches in affected cat indifference and licked at his flanks in grotesque postures, sprang high, scuttled away as others prowled near.

King's hardy confidence that had sunk closer to despair than he cared to admit needed no more than that small mushroom of hope to swell to its normal alert preparedness.

"Three to eleven. We unarmed. That's odds a little stiffer than I had hoped. But I don't see how it could be any different here. Watch that beautiful little devil. Watch the craft of him. By golly, I'll buy him six wives for this."

THE LITTLE leopard's craft was apparent in his gamboling ever closer to the prison cage. He would stop in the moonlight and peer into the darkness of the door; he would sniff as though scenting mice. Once, when the clearing emptied of dancers, he slipped close and was instantly swallowed into the black shadow of the hut.

"Aa-ah!" King tightened all over. But a leopard man raced out of his hiding to meet another in mid clearing. Others pranced into the mêlée. The smallest leopard skipped away to gambol around them.

Twice again it happened. Twice within the next twenty crawling minutes the clearing emptied of cats and twice the mice held their breath. But each time the little one was prowling just too far to make use of his chance.

Those were the most excruciating minutes of the whole imprisonment to King. It was the warm stickiness of his hands that let him know that he must have been straining at his bonds until the coarse grass rope had rasped his wrists to bleeding. An awful thought assailed him that the thing was by design: that the cats cunningly knew and that, sure of their mice, this was exquisite refinement of their play. The wetness that oozed down his face from his forehead was salty on his dry lips.

When it came, it was without any preparation of tightening nerves, with the sudden silent ferocity of a leopard's pounce.

King did not even know that the clearing was empty. All he knew was that one of the guards in the outer dark grunted a startled question to which the answer was the soft hiss of metal piercing flesh, followed instantly by a muted gasp, and then the sound of limbs subsiding on hard packed earth.

Then out of the darkness on the other side of the doorway came an astonished challenge. "*Mtu yupi? Kunani?* Who's that? What's happening?" Followed quickly a repetition of the swift blade to flesh.

The doorway darkened to a quickly ducking shape and the Hottentot's voice came, vibrant with a fierce satisfaction.

"This time I was hiding in the shadow of the hut." And a wailing little cry. "It is well, *Bwana?* Are you in condition to fight, *Bwana?*"

Before King could reply the Hottentot had nosed him out like a dog and was whimpering as he felt for lashings to be cut.

King was laughing softly, the low crackling laughter of relief, of action after near despair.

"It is well done, little Apeling. Now loose the other one." He was flexing his fingers and stretching his shoulders. "Where is now Barounggo?"

The moon-speckled clearing was alive again with posturing, leaping, cat shapes, too preoccupied with their play to discern in the black shadow of their mouse trap that guards slumped on the ground rather than stood upright.

"Barounggo," the Hottentot said, as pleased as a small child, reporting obedience, "is already on his way with the wagon to the Ndolia country, as *Bwana* ordered."

Ponsonby's whisper was tensely urgent over his shoulder. "D'you think, old man, we'll have a chance to sneak out the next time they go into hiding?"

"Not one in a million," King said with a cheerful finality that was surging to high tide after its depression.

Kaffa's dark form ducked out of the doorway, ducked immediately back. "Their two spears, *Bwana*. The sowing of Barounggo's many lessons to *Bwana* will now bear red fruit, and my knife has already learned the road to silence. It is enough. And the glass eye might also be of some small help. Let us go swiftly before ill fate leads one to look close."

"Aa-ah!" King slid his hands along the spear haft in the dark to feel out its balance. "Not a chance to sneak out," he repeated to Ponsonby. "But a damned fine chance to fight out. We're white men armed again."

His laugh barked out. "Here's where we get our chance, Britisher, to show how good our white man superiority is when it's even weapons both ways." And he was suddenly very grim. "And here's where you learn what it feels like to hope to God this still isn't some of your Piet Vreeden's trading. Anyway, remember they're masked coyotes, and a spear handles like a bayonet more or less, only there's more science to it. Come on, Kaffa! Now is as good as any time."

HE SLIPPED through the doorway and stood for just a moment in the shadow to orient the whole scene.

Two leopard men grappled in mimicry of the disemboweling tactic. A third poised, ready to leap in on the loser. Others prowled or posed as the moment, caught them.

King raced out into the moonlight, straight for the group of three. Not a fleeting compunction troubled him about taking them at their disadvantage. Destruction was his single purpose. Plain slaughter, as fast and as efficient as might be.

The man poised above the grapplers looked up in time to let out a hoarse yelp and to leap high and away with all the instant, steel spring agility of a cat. But King's lunge to the full reach of his own long arm and spear drove low into the man's belly in mid leap. He screamed once and dropped to roll over and over, doubled up in the shadows. The two grapplers, wretched fellows, were still twisting apart when the broad spear head stabbed down at the one. The other one's screeching was a caterwaul of frenzy as he fought to free himself from his fellow's convulsed clutch. King grunted his effort to wrench his blade out of the quivering back and chest and grunted again to heave up and pin the fellow hard to the ground.

Ponsonby's shout came, astoundingly true to form. "Yoicks and awa-ay!"

"Attaboy!" King yelled his own excitement and encouragement. "Coyotes are like foxes!"

He dragged his blade free in time to turn and see Ponsonby inexpertly tugging to clear his spear from the side of a man who reeled drunkenly about and screamed, to see another leopard man rushing at Ponsonby with a ready spear—to see the Hottentot, running like a baboon in the half dark, converge upon the spearman, leap high to his shoulders and hack at him with his knife.

Quick padding steps claimed his immediate attention. A long limbed fellow came at him, his teeth snarling white under the great fangs of his leopard mask. Spearless—that one was brave enough—he snarled rage and lashed out at King's neck with steel claws that flashed a vicious arc in the moon beam.

Just turned, King was off balance. The best that he could do was what a white man must do in a fight, duck close and clinch. The fellow's wrist, instead of his claws, smacked hard against

King's jugular vein. And then he was King's meat. The claws raked King's back as King pressed close and drove his free fist at the man's diaphragm. The man retched an agonized grunt and fell away, doubled up with his hands to his belly and gasping. King ruthlessly speared him as he reeled.

And then, all of a sudden, the screeching, snarling fury of fight was gone. There were no more cats.

The moon flickered its pale tracery of shadows on an empty clearing. There was Ponsonby, looking about him in a dazed sort of manner. And there was Kaffa, insatiate, cautiously edging his way into the big house.

"One went in here," he explained over his shoulder. A moon patch on the door post showed the white of his little teeth and his rolling eyes, avid for the hunt.

"Out, you little fool!" King shouted at him. "Cut it out! That's too much of a chance!"

The little devil was too intent upon the hunt to obey.

"Nay, *Bwana*." His voice came muffled from the doorway's blackness. "*Bwana* forgets that a Hottentot can see in the dark much better than any imitation leopard. Hold the door, till I chase him."

But the Hottentot did not chase the man out. Instead, there was a screech that lifted King's stomach up to his throat. And then Kaffa came out alone.

"It was easy," he said. "That would be leopard was very much afraid."

King looked warily around. There was nothing. Even the jungle creatures crouched, silenced for the moment.

"Well then," King said. "Let's show our smartness by running like hell. You lead, Kaffa, to pick the path. You next, Ponsonby. I'm rear guard, though I'm thinking there'll hardly be any need."

There was little talking for an hour after that. But, as stinging thorn twigs sprang back in the broken light and raked faces, there was some cursing whole hearted enough to show that spirits rode high with the moon.

Clear out of the twisty thorn scrub at last, King asked: "How many did you get, Apeling?"

"Only two, *Bwana.*" The Hottentot clucked dissatisfaction with himself. "For the two guards, taken unawares, can hardly count. But the one in the house should count as a good credit."

"Credit, rather, for your coming, Apeling, which will surely not be forgotten. And Ponsonby got one." King saw no cause for dissatisfaction. "Three to nine. How's that for a credit to white man superiority—when a good African helps? Anyway, I think it'll be some time before the remaining pair of leopards will reorganize the local union. Still, we'd better put ground between us. All you've got to worry about, now, Britisher, is that your feet hold out."

AT THE Ndolia mission was the wagon and the Masai, grinning and inhaling unnecessarily great quantities of snuff that made his eyes water. He spat into his two hands and knelt to lay them on his master's feet.

"When *Bwana* is washed and fed," he said, "the tale of the slaughter will be a good telling over the fire. And when *Bwana* is rested it will be well that we go back into that country and exact a vengeance for the insult."

But while the Bwanas splashed hot water over their naked bodies out of a five-gallon kerosene can under a tree, King grinned over to Ponsonby and said:

"Well, Britisher, I guess you've got a mouthful to tell your fat bosses about steel when you get back to your job."

Ponsonby's face remained stolidly serious.

"I have no job," he said. "I resigned from that, er—that sort of business while I was still a mouse in a cage."

"Good for you! That's something for congratulation."

"Thanks, old chap. And I'll tell you what." Ponsonby was characteristically diffident in the presence of money. It was effort to make himself say it.

"I have a few pounds saved up and, er—that is, if you don't

mind, you know—I'd like to buy in your wagon load and get back in there and—"The absence of a monocle to polish embarrassed him horribly. "I'm sort of—what I mean, a fellow ought to go back and trade those chappies good steel for the stuff a fellow has shipped into them, what?"

"Hunh?" King stared.

"I mean it, old man. New lamps for old, if you know what I mean. Sort of take over Vreedon's territory and, er—disinfect it, as you said."

Ponsonby's face was dripping water so that his expression was not entirely easy to read. But it seemed to King, if he could have believed the man capable of humor, that Ponsonby almost grinned through the wetness.

"That is to say, old top, if you have the patience to lead a tenderfoot back and—sort of break me into the new business."

It was King who was serious.

"I think, old chappie," he said, "you're trying to spoof me. But—" He reached out a wet hand. "I figured you'd turn out useful. It's a deal."